We're i... bedroom later, nice and warm from the shower, naked and relaxed on the bed while we watch TV. I'm lying next to Paul, sort of curled around him, and he's sitting at the end of the bed with Jamie at his feet. He's brushing Jamie's hair.

Jamie's hair is at that stage where it's almost dry but still cool and silky and I'm almost mesmerized by the strokes as Paul brushes it. He uses long strokes, starts at the top of Jamie's head and pulls so slowly down to the ends. Jamie's hair is long enough that he leans back a little with each stroke and the swaying of his body is almost putting me to sleep. He's got a nice slow rhythm and I can hear the whispering sound the brush makes through Jamie's hair; soft and soothing.

The brush in Paul's hand pulls the hair away from Jamie, up Paul's body where it falls in a wave over his chest, sliding down his body. It's like a heavy curtain made of tiny threads, and Paul leans forward as it trails down his stomach, and reaches the brush out again to Jamie's head, starting over.

Jamie is sort of rocking with the motion, same was Paul, and I'm feeling kinda sleepy, but a little left out, so I get up and go to the dresser, get another hairbrush so I can do my own.

I turn around to walk back and stop cold.

Gemini
TOP SHELF
An imprint of Torquere Press Publishers
PO Box 2545
Round Rock, TX 78680
Copyright 2005 Chris Owen
Cover illustration by SA Clements
Published with permission
ISBN: 978-1-60370-603-2, 1-60370-603-8
www.torquerepress.com

First Torquere Press Printing: January 2009
Printed in the USA

**If you enjoyed Gemini,
you might enjoy these Torquere Press titles:**

Bareback by Chris Owen

Sex, Lies and Celluloid by Chris Owen and Jodi Payne

Spiked by Mychael Black, Laney Cairo, Jourdan Lane, and Willa Okati

Velvet Glove, Volume III by Sean Michael

Gemini

Chris Owen

Gemini
by Chris Owen

Torquere
Press
Inc.
romance for the rest of us
www.torquerepress.com

Gemini

Chapter One

S o, I'm at work last night, just doing my shit. Clearing out a bunch of old tat mags, trying to keep the place from being an utter dump, when this guy comes in. I'm watching him out of the corner of my eye as he checks the place out, and I'm wondering what the fuck he's in here for. He's doing all the right 'new to tattoo parlor' shit, looking at the health inspection certs and stuff, but he just looks so wrong in here.

He's real tight-laced looking, wearing jeans and sneakers, and this t-shirt that looks like it was ironed; not a wrinkle or loose bit about him. He's got light hair, cut real short, and he looks like he'd be more comfortable in a lecture hall somewhere discussing politics. Municipal politics.

I finish sorting the mags and watch him looking at some art on the walls. Celtic stuff, intricate knot work. Not the thick bands, but delicate tats that take some time and are totally worth the effort. He's about my age, I think, but he looks way younger, really soft around the edges. And he looks so scared, I wonder if he's about to piss himself.

So I wander over and look at the flash with him. I point to one of the knots, a lacy vine thing that is gorgeous and not as girly as it sounds. "That's a nice one."

He looks and me and nods, gives me this shy smile. He's got green eyes.

"Yeah. Not here for art though. Got an appointment with Bobby in about five minutes."

I blink and look him over. Bobby is the piercer, and I've got this guy figured for maybe an eyebrow ring—something to scare his parents with, but nothing too exotic.

"Yeah?" I say, "What're you getting done?" I kind of quirk an eyebrow at him, trying to look friendly 'cause he's hot. Still, I'm not really picturing this guy going in for body mods.

He kind of looks away from me for a second, then back. "Nipple."

And I can't help it, I grin and bring my hand up to my chest and press my shirt tight, showing my own off. "Hey, you should get them both done," I say and wonder why the hell I'm saying it. Then my mouth keeps talking. "Then you can link them with a chain, like I do. Feels real cool."

His eyes get a little wild and he looks me up and down, then grins. "Can I see?"

So what do I do? I lift my shirt for the pretty boy. Not sure where my brain is at this point. I've got rings in both nipples and this fine gold chain linking them. He's staring at my chest and I can feel myself start to get hard, 'cause, well, I'm me. Then he reaches a hand out to me, and pulls it back.

"Go ahead," I say. Shy always gets to me—I think it's a personality flaw. Maybe.

He reaches out to me again and fingers the chain lightly,

then steps a little closer and tugs on it. He's holding my eyes and he's working the chain like he knows exactly what it's doing to me, sending bolts of fucking fire to my cock, and then he says, real quiet, "Like that, do you?"

I nod and try to grin, but he's looking me up and down, real slow and his eyes are hot and I can see he's getting hard in his jeans.

Bobby sticks his head out the door and calls him, so he lets go of my chain and smiles at me. Says, "Yeah, maybe I'll do both." Then he's gone.

I go to the desk and hunt up his release form. His name is Paul and I was right, he's my age. Exactly. We share a birthday.

When he comes out he's got both nipples done and orders to keep a chain off until they heal. When he leaves he's got a business card with my name and number on the back.

So he didn't call. No big, wasn't really thinking he would. He was pretty though, and he was into me, I thought. Little disappointing, but I guess that just shows that I'm lonely and a sucker for pretty boys with green eyes who look like they're needing to be debauched.

Then I was at work, about three weeks later, right about the supper rush time. It's amazing how many people stop in on a weeknight on their way home from work, just to look at the art on the walls, or talk about mods. Anyway, I was at the desk, booking in this chick who was having trouble deciding between this fairy with anime eyes or a classic dolphin for her ankle. I'm being nice to her, setting up the appointment and shit, but I'm thinking "Christ, lady, this is fucking permanent ink, you're gonna have it for a long time. A tat should mean something to you, not be a pretty little whim that you put on." I mean, I do the inking, but shit, I only have two tats myself. Mind you, they're pretty fucking mind bending. I just get so sick of people coming in and picking something from the wall just 'cause they want a tattoo. People have actually told me that they just want one because so and so has one, and everyone else does, too.

The ones I really like are the ones people design for themselves. I've seen some pretty crappy artwork, but if the person wants it and has taken the time to create an image for themselves...that's cool.

Where was I? Oh, right, dolphin chick. So, I'm booking her in and I look up and see Paul, leaning against the wall watching me. I grin at him and finish up with the lady, and then walk over to him. He's wearing fucking slacks and a button-down shirt. And dress shoes.

"Hey, Paul. You just off work?" I ask.

"Yeah. How are you doing, Gent?" He smiles at me, pretty shy but sweet, too, and his eyes are warm. So I forgive him for not calling.

"'M good," I say. "How's the piercing? Healing okay?" There's people fucking everywhere, moving around us and looking like they need help. I'm just ignoring them, moving closer to Paul.

"It's good," he says and nods. Then he looks right at me and sort of licks his lips, looking nervous all of a sudden. Before, he was just leaning on the wall, now he's more bracing himself than leaning and I move closer, not sure what he wants, but hey, I'm me. I can hope.

"Uh, was just wondering when you finish up here for the night," he says, his eyes looking away and then back to me, real fast. "Wondered if maybe you wanted to go for a drink or something. Shoot some pool. Whatever."

I smile at him, and nod. "Yeah, that'd be cool. Not done until about ten though, is that okay?"

He smiles back, a little flushed, and it's just so damn sweet. "No, not a problem. I'll come back then, if that's..."

"Yeah, that's okay. Very." I'm in his personal space now, and he's not looking like he minds. I'm even thinking that I might try a move, something small, but then Bobby, Goddamn him, is hollering for me to get my ass to the desk.

"I'll see ya later then," I say and move away.

"Yeah. Later."

Paul comes back just at ten when Bobby's flipping the sign to closed. He tries to wave Paul away, so I just say, "Hey, let him in. We're gonna go shoot some stick."

Bobby looks at me, sort of like What the hell are you thinking?, and I just grin at him. He lets Paul in and comes over to me. "He's not your type, Gent."

I grin at him again. "Why not?"

Bobby rolls his eyes. "Straighter than a ruler, idiot."

"Hey, he asked me." Yeah, I smirk and look at Paul out of the corner of my eye. Damn, he looks good. He's changed his clothes and now he's got on dark pants, kind of loose but not baggy, and a leather jacket. Nice black leather, well worn.

Bobby just shrugs and moves away so I go over to the wall where Paul's looking at art. I hold his arm, just above the elbow, and he turns to look at me. God, those eyes of his are just so fucking green.

"Hey," I say. "You ready to go?"

He nods and kind of tilts his head to the side and I can see his skin start to flush. I slide my hand down his arm and he takes my hand as we leave.

We walk down the street like that, just taking about

shit. Find out he works at City Hall, and doesn't that just make sense. I tell him we have the same birthday and we talk about the differences in time zones until we figure out that he's about six hours older than me. He knows to the minute when he was born, but I just have an approximate hour.

"So," I say as we wander down a street, "You want to drink? Play pool? Whatever?"

He grins and says, "Yeah."

Yeah, he's into me. Cool.

We go into this bar I know, a dark little place called the Razor's Edge, and since it's early there's almost no one there. Taff, the guy at the bar, just hands me my beer and raises an eyebrow at Paul, who nods and gets the same. We walk over to the pool tables and he takes off the jacket and I swear I just about pass out. He's got this fucking tight black t-shirt on and I can see his nipple rings clear as shit. I get hard just looking at him.

We shoot a couple games of pool and I think he's nervous, 'cause he loses the first one real bad. He wins the second one though. Maybe because my cock is throbbing and I can't see to line up the shots properly. Or maybe he's just better at pool when he's had a beer.

He's lining up to break for the third game and I finish my beer, then go stand behind him, lean over and put my hand on the cue. He pushes back into me, and glances over his shoulder, with this wicked grin that makes my cock leap. He scratches on purpose and turns around, pretty much right into my arms.

"Whoops. Is it time for whatever now?" he asks, one hand landing on my hip.

"Fuck, yes. C'mon." I lead him out of the bar, trying to figure out where the hell to go, and he grabs me from behind and pulls me in the other direction, away from the street. We go down the alley and around a corner, and then he's got me up against the wall, his mouth on mine.

He tastes like beer and toothpaste, and something else. Not sure what, don't care. I can feel his prick against mine as he grinds me into the wall.

"Oh yeah," I manage as he pulls back and undoes my pants. "Touch me." His breath is hot on my skin and I'm pretty much panting for it.

He's got my cock out and in his hand, pulling at me with one fist as his other hand goes in my shirt and finds my chain. He plays with it a bit and moans when I work my hand into his pants, feel his dick hot in my hand.

He's kissing me and jerking me off, one hand teasing my nipple rings and I'm about to blow right there in some scummy alley.

"Christ, you're a surprise," I gasp as he sweeps his fingers over me, pulling hard and fast.

He grins and then swears as I do the same to him.

"You got anything?" I ask. "Not gonna last long." I really want to fuck, my hips are pushing, his are slamming against me, and I just want the real thing.

He shakes his head and thrusts into my fist. "No—I don't, I didn't usually do—oh God, I'm gonna come—"

I kiss him hard, thinking that it doesn't matter if we have anything, 'cause there's no way we can stop and we're just gonna have to settle for a quick hand job in an alley, fuck later, and then he shudders in my arms and shoots his load over my hand. I feel it hit my cock and that's it. I fucking cry out something, I don't know what, and then I shoot, too, all over us both.

We stand there panting for a bit and then try to clean up as best we can. I look at him, worried about what he's gonna think. He pretty much said that he hadn't planned on a quickie and I sure as hell hadn't, but I like him and don't want him running away.

It seems to be okay though, because he grins at me and

kisses me, quick and hard, completely jazzed. "Fuck, that needs a follow-up."

I grin back and we start walking, not really caring where.

I keep looking at him. He's happy and relaxed and just 'Paul after being almost fucked'. I like it.

"So, how do you like your nipple rings?" I ask, more for something to say than anything else.

"Like 'em a lot. Got them as a surprise for a guy." He looks at me, his eyes suddenly weird. Sort of searching, sort of hopeful, sort of scared.

"He didn't like them?" Stupid idiot, not liking Paul with pierced nipples. His loss, my gain.

"He likes them fine," he says, his voice real quiet and hesitant.

I stop walking. "What the fuck? You're with someone and you do that with me?" Yeah, from happy and horny me to pissed off me in two seconds. You better fucking believe it.

"I'll be with him forever," Paul says and moves in front of me, staring into my eyes, trying to tell me something I don't get. "His name's Jamie. He's my twin."

I try to say 'What the fuck?' again, but what comes out is "I beg your pardon?"

Paul's staring at me, and I can't read his eyes. He's telling me that he and his brother... well, Goddamn. He's not saying anything, just looking at me with those green eyes, and I think I'm seeing hope.

"You and your twin... you—?" I don't know what else to say. He nods at me, still staring, watching my face. "That's just so not what I was expecting." And whoa, is it hot, part of my brain yells out. I tell it to shut up.

I walk away a bit and he's right beside me, not saying anything.

"Paul, I don't know if I can do that," I finally say,

looking at my feet. "I mean be with you and have you be with him, too." I look at him and he's shaking his head.

"It's not like that, it's – fuck, I knew I should have listened to him. Jamie said not to tell you until later, but if this is gonna work right you gotta know now."

"He knows you're out with me and he's okay with that?" I'm not sure why that's the surprising part, but to me it is.

Paul stops walking and we're standing there on the sidewalk, facing each other. Like we're having a normal conversation instead of talking about him and his twin, and oh Christ, what is wrong with me that the very thought of it is making me hard again?

"We—we had a lover, for a long time. Three can work well, it's just a matter of finding the right three, and—"

I interrupt him. "Yeah, I get that, three doesn't bother me." And it doesn't. Really. Three can work fine, I've seen it. "I'm not too sure about the twin thing though. I mean fuck, that's just too fucking much to think about." That part of my brain I told to shut up? It's sing-songing 'too fucking hot' at me. Stupid brain.

He nods and we start walking. "He wants to meet you."

"What?" Okay, now I'm just floundering, completely out of my depth.

"I haven't shut up about you for three weeks, and Jamie says that if you're that hot and if things go okay tonight, he'd like to meet you." He's really matter of fact about it, which I think is good. Someone has to be normal about the sheer abnormality of this, and I'm thinking it's not me.

So we walk. And I think. And I'm all confused. This is just so... not what I was expecting. Easy to walk away now. Would have been easier before tonight, before we talked and got all twisted in the alley. And I can't get this picture out of my head, him and someone who looks like just like him, going at it. Fuck.

"Identical?" I want to stab out my eye. Why does my mouth do that?

Paul smiles, kind of dreamy. "Yeah. His hair is longer though, and real soft."

So I sigh and say, "Yeah, okay. Not promising anything, but what the fuck."

He grins at me and suddenly I think that this is going to be a very long night.

Chapter Two

We get to this building, one of those ones that look like utter shit outside but is full of reclaimed space. Up the elevator and into a fucking palace. High ceilings, lots of windows, and just space.

"Wow. Who all lives here? It's huge," I say, wandering around this big room full of overstuffed furniture and low tables.

"Just me and Jamie. We inherited it when our parents died."

I glance at him and he's smiling at me, watching me move through the room. "Want a drink? Kitchen's that way."

I follow him to the kitchen and sit down while he pulls a couple of beers out of the fridge. He hands one to me and leans back against the fridge, just smiling a little.

I don't have a fucking clue what to say.

"Jamie's out. Playing ball, I think. But he should be back any time."

I nod and just watch him. I still feel completely out of my depth, but he's just Paul, looking nervous and shy, which is just strange at this point. He's fucking got my come on his shirt and I look down at myself, see the stains on my own clothes. I glance up and he's grinning, and it really is kinda funny so I smile back.

"You two do this a lot?" I ask, 'cause I gotta know. In my head I'm adding up twins and guys and viruses and it's not looking so good.

"Do what?" He looks confused, and I guess he doesn't have a clue what I'm on about.

"Bring home other guys to play with." Man, that sounds bad just laid out like that, but it is what it is, and I'm not going to play stupid.

His face clears. "No. We don't. Like I said, there was someone but he left about a year ago. He was with us for three years, and before him there wasn't anybody. Not even Jamie." He's looking at me real serious, like he really wants me to understand. "The three of us sort of happened, and it worked. Then he left, and it was just us."

I raise a brow. "Why me? Why now?"

Paul shifts and looks down, and I can see an honest to fucking God blush creep up his face. "Wanted you," he mumbles.

I was gonna say something, but then the front door opens and closes out in the other room and a voice calls out, "Paul? You home?"

"Kitchen!" Paul calls back, not moving.

This guy walks in, looking just like Paul except his hair is long, longer than mine even, and pulled back in a ponytail. He's wearing a t-shirt and cut off sweatpants.

Oh fuck, I am so done.

He stops when he sees me and looks at Paul, one eyebrow up. Paul nods and Jamie turns to me and smiles. Same fucking sweet shy smile Paul has, but a bit more... vibrant, maybe. "Hey. I'm Jamie."

I smile back and say, "Gent."

Jamie moves through the kitchen, heading to the cupboards just past the refrigerator. "You guys shoot some pool tonight?"

I say, "Yeah. Tied out at one game apiece."

He grins and reaches up for a glass and brushes past Paul. If I wasn't watching for it, didn't know that they were fucking, I would have missed it. But I saw. Saw him flick a finger over Paul's nipple ring, saw Paul suck in air, saw Jamie shift and smile at him. Then it was over and they were apart.

"Have a good time, Paul?" he asks, getting some water from the sink.

Paul looks at me and says, "Yeah. Real good."

Jamie steps away from the sink and takes a good look at his twin and I can see his eyes widen at the stains. Then he smirks at him and grins at me. "Yeah, I guess you did. I'll leave you to it then." He starts to leave the kitchen.

"I told him." Paul's voice is soft, just above a whisper, but Jamie freezes and I see the muscles in his back working.

He turns around and looks at me, really looks. He smiles then, more cautiously than before, and says, "Well, you're here. That says something anyway." He comes over and sits down at the table and looks at me expectantly. Studying me.

I have no fucking idea what I'm supposed to do.

Jamie looks at Paul. "Like him?" he asks frankly.

Paul nods and gives me that shy smile again. "Yeah."

Jamie just settles back and looks at him. I think I've been dismissed.

"Talk to me, Paul."

So Paul talks. It's really weird, sitting there while Paul pretty much relays an hour and half of conversation in a few minutes. Tells Jamie what movies I like, what books

I like to read, how long I've been inking. Tells him we all share a birthday, and that makes Jamie grin at me. Paul's saying stuff about me that I didn't even think I'd let out, like how I wanted to be an artist but my dad discouraged it, and how I'd thought art school wasn't for me 'cause I didn't really care about art history, but that I'd gone anyway and found out I was more into the academic side of it than I'd thought, although learning to copy someone else's technique seemed silly to me, and a bunch of other stuff. That I'm serious and intense, but funny, too, which is a bit of a surprise to me—I'm not funny. He says that I look him in the eye when he talks, but I say more with my posture and my hands than I do with words. Tells him about playing pool, and what my eyes did when he took off his jacket.

Jamie looks at me. "What do you think?"

I just shake my head and say, "I have no clue what to think. This is different, you know? Don't know."

He nods. "Yeah. For us, too. Never actively brought anyone in before. But I can tell you that if you just want to get your rocks off and say you were with twins you can go find yourself another set. I know Paul. He's into you. You want to see him, we're pretty much a package deal."

I translate this to mean, 'I share, but I'm not leaving, so don't even think it.' I look at Paul and he's watching me. Look at Jamie, see that his eyes are green, too, but a bit browner. Need the difference.

"Don't know you," I finally say.

He smiles and nods. "Yeah, I don't know you either."

Then we're all smiling, and I don't know why. Jamie stands up and goes over to Paul, stands right in front of him. Jamie has a hand on the back of Paul's head and he leans in, presses their foreheads together. His other hand is tracing the stains on Paul's pants and shirt. "Ya wanna tell me how you got these?"

Paul puts an arm over Jamie's shoulder and kisses him, deep. I just stare. They're moving together, their hips rocking gently as Jamie's fingers keep tracing the patterns I made on Paul's clothes, kissing like they were trying to get into each other's skins.

And I'm sitting there on a kitchen chair getting harder and harder, wondering if I can just rub myself off through my jeans while I watch.

"Tell me about it, Paul. Make me see." Jamie's voice is low and husky, I can barely hear him from three feet away.

Paul looks at him, eyes shining, and then he glances at me, his smile less shy and sweet and more 'hey, watch what I can do'. He winks at me and pulls Jamie tight to him.

"Had him in an alley, Jamie, couldn't wait, didn't want to go anywhere, just needed to kiss him, touch him. Pushed him up against the wall."

Jamie moans and leans in more, forcing Paul into the fridge. "Like this?"

Paul kisses him and slips a hand under the waistband of Jamie's sweatpants, at the back so I can see. "Yeah, like this. Kissed him hard, he tasted like beer and something rich and deep. God, it's a great taste, Jamie. Needed him so bad, I was so fucking hard for him."

Jamie grinds into him and they both make some noise. I drop a hand to my lap and push at the base of my cock.

"Had a hand up his shirt to touch his chain, a hand in his pants jerking him off."

Jamie does to Paul what Paul's telling him, and it's my turn to whimper. They are so fucking hot together. Theory is one thing, and who hasn't had a secret fantasy about two at once, or even about twins? If you're into twins, these two could blow your mind. It suddenly dawns on me that this whole thing with Jamie is a sort of test, 'see how Gent reacts to twin action'. I'm not minding in the least, moving around on the chair, eyes fucking glued to Jamie's hands on Paul, to Paul's hand moving around to the front of Jamie's sweatpants, pulling them down where it's important.

"Yeah, like that Jamie," Paul says, his voice husky. "I was so fucking hard and his hand was hot and firm and his cock was heavy in my hand and I just wanted to fuck him right there in the alley, spin him around and push my way inside."

Someone moans, I think it's me. The twins are up against the fridge all over each other, kissing and humping and moaning and, oh fuck, it's hot. They've got each other's cocks out and are stroking and touching and I can't fucking take it. I pop the button on my jeans and shove my hand in my pants, start to jerk off there in the kitchen.

Paul pins those green eyes on me and sees what I'm doing. He gasps and thrusts hard into Jamie's hand and his eyes roll back in his head. I'm waiting for him to come, trying to get there at the same time, but he doesn't.

When he opens his eyes again he tears his mouth away from Jamie's and says, "C'mere, Gent."

Jamie moans something into Paul's neck and I get up, still stroking off, and go over to them, plaster myself to Jamie's back. I push against him, lean in to kiss Paul and then Jamie turns his head to kiss me, too, and I can suddenly taste the differences in them, Jamie more coffee than chocolate, a darker flavour, just as smooth as Paul.

They're humping and stroking and Jamie wraps an arm back around my waist, pulling me into him and all I can do is move with them, rubbing my prick up against Jamie's ass, my hands around his chest, one teasing at his nipples and the other joining his hands up Paul's shirt, playing with a nipple ring. I show Jamie what I like, just tug gently on Paul's ring, hoping it has the same effect for him as it does for me, and, fuck does it ever.

Paul throws his head back and shoots, coming all over Jamie's hand and cock, and Jamie thrusts his tongue into my mouth and I feel him gasp, more than I hear him. Jamie comes hard, shaking in my arms and kisses me just as hard, his tongue fucking my mouth and they are just so unbelievably hot together.

It's Jamie who sends me over. His mouth on mine, his ass against my hard prick, him in my arms and his voice, low and deep, growling into my mouth, "Want you."

I shoot, spraying come up his fucking back.

Oh God. I think I could like this.

Chapter Three

We take a shower, just getting clean, and then we tumble into bed. I swear Paul's asleep before he can get the alarm set and kiss us both goodnight. He says I love you to Jamie and goodnight to me and then he's gone.

We're all spooned together on the bed, me in the middle with Jamie behind me. He's got one arm over me, reaching all the way over to hold onto Paul too, and it's nice and warm.

"Hey," Jamie whispers in my ear.

"Hey," I whisper back.

"You cool with this?"

I grin, know he can't see it. "Seem to be," I say and wiggle my butt against him.

He laughs softly and I feel his hand in my hair. "Yeah." He pauses, just playing with my hair for a minute or so. "You wanna get lunch tomorrow? While Paul's at work, I mean. We can talk and shit, get to know each other a little."

I nod. "Yeah, that'd be cool. Have to do it early

though, I gotta work at one."

He shifts behind me and I can feel him getting hard.

"Yeah, that's okay. I don't have to work until three."

"Where do you work?" I ask, moving back a bit, just rocking into his growing hard-on.

"Downtown. Manage a bookstore. Should be Paul's job, but he freaking loves it at City Hall, and I like the store okay. Gotta close one night a week though, and tomorrow's it." He's moving harder into me, and he's real fucking hard now. God, he gets hard fast.

"Cool," I say, and I can feel my own cock trying to match his and wonder when the hell I turned into Superman.

"Love your hair," he whispers, his fingers sliding through it. "Love it loose like this, so dark on the pillow, clean and soft and long."

I nod, agreeing with him. Like Paul's hair fine, but Jamie's is longer than mine, and wavy and like silk.

"Can I fuck you?" he breathes into my ear.

I shiver and moan and turn my head to kiss him, saying yes with my tongue. We let go of Paul and shift over on the bed and kiss for a bit, nice deep hungry kisses. Jamie finally breaks away, his eyes glazing over and his breath shallow. He gets a condom and lube from the nightstand and I lay on my back, spreading my legs for him.

We don't talk, just move together. I haven't been with anyone like this in what feels like ages, though it's probably only been a couple of months. He gets me ready fast, long fingers stretching me and then he's inside, filling me and I realize he's got a big fucking cock, nice and wide.

He moves fast, short thrusts that have my head spinning as he kisses me, his cock deep in me and we're moaning and grinding together, my prick trapped between us, getting just enough friction, but not enough to come.

Jamie props himself up on his arms and keeps his hips

moving, the head of his cock finding my prostate, and I groan. He smiles and does it again, moving inside me like he fucking owns me, and he dips his head, playing at my nipple rings with his tongue.

"Oh God, yes," I breathe, then I can't even speak as he rubs over my gland again and again and tugs at my chain with his teeth.

"Fuck, Gent," he whispers. "So hot. Paul was right, you're so intense, gonna make you come for me." He's got me on the edge and I can feel it in my spine, in the back of my head, fucking everywhere. I spread my legs more, draw up my knees, opening to him.

He gasps and then fucks me hard, his hips slamming down and I'm thrusting up, riding him, getting so fucking close, needing just a little more to go over. He's got all his weight on his hands, kissing me again, and I reach down to pull at my cock and he moans.

"Yeah, Gent, like that, do it for me. Come for me."

I groan and thrust up harder, taking him deep while my hand fists my cock and I grab his ass with the other hand, hold him deep in me while I come, spunk hitting my stomach and chest.

"Oh God, yes!" he cries out, loud enough to wake Paul, and he's coming in me.

We're riding it out, still moving together when Paul rolls over. His eyes are sleepy and he looks at us for a few seconds before figuring it out.

"You two getting along?" he asks finally.

"Yeah," Jamie says with a grin before kissing me again.

"Good," Paul says, and then he rolls over and goes back to sleep.

Lunch with Jamie was cool. He's more into sports shit than I am, but I like hockey so we talked about that for a while. We talked about art, too, and some books we'd both read, and Paul.

When we'd had enough to eat we went back to the apartment so I could get my coat and then head off to work. And yeah, I like him fine. He's funny, has a weird sense of humour, and he loves Paul. And he's really hot.

We walk into the place and I get my jacket from the couch. When I turn around he's just looking at me, eyes hot, and I cross to him in about three strides, kiss him hard as we fall into chair, hands everywhere.

"I'm gonna be late for work," I say as he works his hand into my pants.

"Yeah."

Then we just work at getting naked. Well, partially naked. His hand's on my cock, and I've got his shirt pulled up and his jeans undone and we're just moving together, not wanting to let go long enough to even strip off. He's kissing me, and it's just so good.

I'm in his lap, which makes it real hard to get to his prick, so I slide off and he has to let go of my cock, which is so not good, but necessary if I'm gonna suck him off. I get to my knees between his thighs and reach for my coat, where it landed on the floor. Then I remember that I don't have any rubbers.

I look up at him and he knows what I'm after. He grins at me and stands up, tugging his pants back up and says, "Bedroom. Race ya." And he's fucking gone.

I know where he is so I take my time, strip off my clothes before going after him. When I get there he's naked, spread out on the bed, lube and condoms beside him.

"So, we know each other well enough now?" I ask, jumping onto the bed and making him bounce in the most wonderful way.

"Yeah, I think so. Kiss me. Then fuck me."

He's laughing and happy and so Goddamn hard. Can't really turn him down.

Kissing Jamie isn't like kissing Paul at all. They taste way different, and where Paul is sort of tentative at first and then gets more aggressive as it goes along, Jamie just dives in, fucking my mouth with his tongue. And it's good. The difference, I mean. And the kissing.

He's got his fingers on my nipple rings and he starts to tug gently, making me catch my breath.

"What's it like?" he asks.

I kinda shrug and then lick at his chest, find a nipple with my mouth and tease it for a bit until it's stiff and hard in my mouth, then I gently pull at it with my teeth. Jamie swears and arches his back, and I grin at him.

"Can see why Paul gets off on them," he says.

I nod and kiss him again, rubbing my cock on his. "So what gets you off?" I ask.

He chuckles into the kiss. "Finding out is half the fun, Gent. Not gonna tell you all my secrets right away."

I laugh and move down his body, snagging a rubber as I go and get it open. I suck at the skin on his belly, amazed at how hard his abs are. He's all tight muscle and smooth skin. I can get lost there, if I let myself.

I get the latex on him and take his cock in my mouth, tease him with my tongue.

"Oh yeah. Feels nice."

I lick at him, moving down his shaft and lick at his balls, pushing his legs open and back, sucking and nuzzling and fucking tasting him. He's rocking with me now, letting me know with his body what he likes. He's starting to breathe faster and I smile, keep licking and sucking, get my fingers wet as I play.

I go back up and suck on the head of his cock and he

moans, tries to thrust into my mouth, but I don't let him. Not yet.

"Please, Gent. C'mon, need it, suck me." He sounds like heaven.

I tease him for a moment longer, run my tongue around the head of his cock until he fucking whimpers. Then I just suck him in and take it all, feel him hit the back of my throat and push it just a little more until I can swallow around him.

"Fuck, yeah!"

Jamie arches into me, and holds my head, pulling my hair. I relax my throat as much as I can and he slips in a little more before losing it and then he's just fucking my mouth. It's all I can do to keep sucking, he's sliding in and out and going as deep as I'll let him and he's swearing and groaning and making the most gorgeous noise.

My balls are hanging loose and I reach a hand down and touch myself, stroke lightly. He sees me, I think, 'cause he slows down a little and moans again.

"Yes, Gent. Do it for me."

I groan around his cock and he shudders, starts thrusting again. I let go of my cock and slide wet fingers over his balls, push his legs back. He cries out when I push two wet fingers into his ass and he's coming for me, thrashing on the bed.

So good.

So hot.

I feel like I'm about to explode, I'm so hard. I suck at him until he's spent and then crawl up to kiss him, thrust against his hip. He's holding onto me and kissing me, and still making soft needy noises and I come all over him, just rub off on his hip and belly and it's good.

I am so fucking late for work.

Chapter Four

Tonight, for the first time, we are all off work from five o'clock on, so we're going to have real food to celebrate. An actual meal, made out of stuff that doesn't come in take-out containers or get delivered at the last minute. Cool.

For the last week or so I've been getting up every morning, doing whoever needs doing, and then going to my own place to change for work. So this morning Jamie gives me his key and tells me to bring some stuff over after work and let myself in. He and Paul are going to go shopping for the food, and then we'll all cook supper. I say great, see ya later, kiss them both and take off.

Work's okay, but kinda slow and my last appointment cancelled. No walk-ins turn up, so I whine at Bobby and Fred until they finally tell me to piss off and go home. I get some shit from my place and make my way to the apartment, get there a little early, 'bout five ten or so.

So I use my key. That's what Jamie lent it to me for, right? So I can let myself in if they aren't back from the store yet. Except they're back. And naked on the living room floor, sucking each other off.

I just about come in my pants and I'm not even hard yet. Or I wasn't until I see that.

I drop my stuff by the door and stumble to the couch, getting my pants undone while I walk. They know I'm there, Jamie sort of looks up at me and grins around Paul's cock then goes back to sucking him off. I strip down and sit on the couch to watch, thinking that this is the hottest thing I've seen in, like, ever.

We've all been together in assorted ways and combinations, but I've never seen them like this before. I've fucked them both, been fucked and sucked and, shit, last night I had Jamie's cock in my ass and Paul's down my throat at the same time, but I've never seen them just together.

They're all warm skin and tight muscles, moving together on the floor, Jamie's hair splayed out all over the place and Paul's making these whimpery noises that mean he's having a blast and loving it all. Thing about Paul is that he seems real tight-laced but the boy is a hedonist and absolutely loves to suck. And he's damn good at it.

I can't see from the couch. Well, I can see, and I can hear, but I want to really see. I want to see Paul's face and Jamie's cock, I want to see Jamie's eyes as he sucks Paul in deep and hard. I move off the couch and crawl over to them, run a hand up Jamie's back and start playing with his hair. He's got gorgeous hair.

Jamie comes off Paul's dick with a slurp and grins at me, reaches a hand to stroke my cock, which makes me moan and makes Paul complain. He wants his mouth back.

"You gonna play?" Jamie asks.

I shake my head. "Nope. Wanna watch your brother swallow you." And then Paul moans, which makes Jamie moan and dive for Paul's prick again, taking him in deep.

Jamie's eyes close and he's starting to thrust with his hips, fucking his twin's mouth and I swear Paul's made of stone, 'cause he's just letting Jamie suck and lick and he's not moving. Jamie has one hand on Paul's hip and the other starts playing with his balls and I'm just sitting there on the floor stroking off.

I lay down next to them, my head near Paul's now and I can see the spark in his eye. The one he got the night he made us both come before he fucked me into the mattress. He's gonna take Jamie's head off.

I watch Paul and I can see when it starts to happen. He sucks a little harder, and on the upstroke he's a little looser, makes Jamie real wet. Fuck, Jamie's so hard, and Paul's working him, tongue everywhere. Then he runs a hand up the inside of Jamie's thigh and he's doing some weird pressure shit to his balls and the soft skin behind them and Jamie's hips are fucking snapping as he tries to get more. I glance back and Jamie's still sucking Paul off, but his rhythm is gone and he's pretty much just licking now.

Paul holds a hand out to me and traces my lips. So I suck his fingers in and let him play, try to match the rhythm he's got going with Jamie. Paul's eyes roll a little and I grin, then he pulls his fingers out of my mouth and fuck he just slides two right up Jamie's ass and Jamie loses it, crying out Paul's name and I can see Paul swallowing hard around Jamie's cock and I think Jamie's never gonna stop coming.

Then Paul's up and off and I'm laying there looking at Jamie who's sprawled on his back and he looks totally fucked. Like he's not getting off the floor for hours.

Paul lands beside me again and kisses me hard, whispers, "Hey. Missed you."

"Yeah?" I say, stroking his erection, and fuck he's

hard.

"Yeah. You still watching, or you want to play yet?"

I grin. "We got all night, baby. Give me a show."

He kisses me again and then he's leaning back, trying to get at a drawer in the coffee table. So I take advantage and lean over him, start to rub off on his abs.

"You want a show, you better stop," he says, and I can hear the grin in his voice. I back off and go to kiss Jamie, which I guess works well for Paul. 'Cause while I'm saying my proper hello's to Jamie his twin found the lube and the next thing I know Jamie's arching up and sucking on my tongue and moaning like he was when Paul had him down his throat.

I look back and down at Paul and drop a hand to my cock, pumping myself hard, 'cause shit, I have never seen anything like this. My twins, my beautiful, gorgeous, sexy twins are fucking for me and Paul's balls deep, Jamie's legs over his arms and he's just fucking slamming into him.

Jamie has to stop kissing me, he just can't hold it together and Paul's looking so determined and hot and oh God I need something, anything.

They're moving together now, hips rolling, and Paul's right over Jamie, kissing him, teasing his chest with the tip of his tongue, and Jamie starts to babble, saying stuff like, "Oh God yes, Paul, fuck me harder. So good, God, you're so hard."

Paul just grins and speeds up, pulling Jamie's legs higher and Jamie's eyes roll back in his head. "Oh shit, yes! Right there, Paul, please, yeah, please!"

I can't just sit through this, can't just jerk off anymore. I'm so hard I hurt and my balls are aching and I need to touch, need to be there with them. I reach out and trace Jamie's cock with one finger and he fucking jerks at my touch and groans, so I fist him and start jerking him off.

Paul's eyes are wide and starting to lose focus, and it's glorious.

Then Paul sort of freezes for a second and Jamie's shooting over my hand and Paul's slamming into him again and then he throws back his head and comes.

And yeah, I give myself another tug and then I shoot all over both of them before we all land in a messy pile, kissing and touching and stroking and just coming down.

We order pizza later.

We're on our way to bed when I remember the key. I kinda pat myself down and finally find it stuck in my back pocket—hell, I don't even remember putting it there. I was a little distracted when I got here. So I put the key on the kitchen counter and grab Jamie as he walks by and cop a quick feel. "Key's here."

He grins at me and looks at the key, wrapping his arms around my waist. "Came in handy, didn't it?" he asks. "Would have been pissed if I'd had to stop to answer the door."

Can't argue with that, can I? I kiss him quickly and hear the TV shut off. Paul's pretty insistent that he watch the late local news if we're not otherwise occupied, so he's the last of us to wander into the kitchen.

"Um, bed's just down the hall," he says, winking at us. "Much more comfortable than the kitchen."

"This from the man who has a thing for the living room floor," I tease, letting Jamie go. "Go on, I need water."

They kind of tumble down the hall, Paul calling Jamie 'insatiable' and Jamie protesting that we weren't actually doing anything, but not really denying the accusation that he can't get enough, either. By the time I get a glass from the cupboard and open the fridge I've heard two thumps as they shoved each other into walls, Paul's grunt as Jamie got him in a headlock, and Jamie's shriek of laughter as Paul wiggled out and started tickling him. It makes me smile—love it when they're silly and brothers.

I get my water and head down the hall, making sure the lights are off. It's weird, you know? I've been spending my time here, been hanging out and, well, honestly, having a hell of a good time and getting off more than I did in the last year, but it's only been a week. I can't remember ever being comfortable like this a week into seeing someone, certainly not doing the whole 'yeah, I'll make sure things are shut off for the night' thing.

I don't really feel like a guest, and it scares the crap out of me.

I walk into the bedroom and find the boys in bed already, laying side by side and grinning at me. There's a gap in the middle of the bed—my spot. I have a spot. It's hard to have a side of the bed when you sleep in the middle, but there it is. My place. I think I'm staring.

"Gent?" Paul asks, looking at me with questions in his eyes. "Something wrong?"

I shake my head slowly. "Nope." And nothing really is, I'm just sort of winded. Suddenly I'm feeling kind of short of breath and utterly freaked the fuck out. What the hell am I doing, and how did I get here?

Jamie and Paul are sitting up in the bed now, looking at each other and then me. "Gent?"

Okay, time to get back to basics. I've got two guys in bed and what I need to know is why. Why me, why them, and why-- why am I here? Aside from the sex. Aside from the twin factor. I mean, I was happy enough just thinking about Paul, wasn't I? Before I knew about Jamie. Okay, granted, that was all of three weeks of daydreams and one brief evening, but still. Paul was enough. I was happy, I think.

And me and Jamie, that's another thing. We get along great. He's funny and forward and just so overwhelming I'm beginning to wonder if I've just been swept away in the newness and hotness of everything. Jamie kind of swept in and captured me, and not that I'm complaining, I'm just wondering, all of a sudden, if I'm really supposed to be here.

They're looking uneasy and mildly freaked, edging closer to each other. I can see them holding hands under the covers, watching me carefully. I feel kind of bad for having my freakout where they can see it, and I'm not stupid—they probably can tell exactly what I'm thinking, or at least guess.

I turn around fast and start pulling off my clothes. I have no clue what to do, or what I'm going to say to calm things down—it's hard to be reassuring when you're in mid-panic. The only thing I really know is that I don't want to walk out. I get the feeling that if I walk now I won't be allowed back in, so where does that leave me?

"Paul?" I ask, tossing my jeans on the chair and getting ready to strip my shorts off.

"Yeah?" Oh, he sounds wary and suspicious and that's not nice. Guilt moves through me, guilt for making him wonder if he made a mistake asking me out in the first place.

Which is what I want to explore. Him asking me out was based on sex, yeah? Attraction. And we had a good time, we talked and started the dating rituals. But we got derailed really fast, and since then there's just been a hell of a lot of orgasms.

Not that orgasms are bad.

Time to get back to the start, I think. So I look at him, as I stand at the foot of the bed, naked and with my dick soft and I ask, "Would you like to go out for supper with me tomorrow night?"

His eyes widen and he smiles at me, nodding. "That'd be nice," he says. Then we both look at Jamie.

He seems to get it, thank Christ. He nods and lays back in the bed, moving a little so I can crawl in. "Good idea," he whispers to me as we curl up. "I'd like to take you out later in the week."

I smile and snuggle down. I'm dating. Neat.

Chapter Five

Dating is kind of cool. Weird and freaky, considering the situation, but... nice. Once or twice a week I have lunch with Jamie, and at least once a week I take Paul out. It's been going on for a while now, maybe a month or so, and we've all been talking our heads off.

Don't get me wrong, there's still plenty of time for the three of us. That's kind of the point, isn't it? We hang out together, sleep together — hell, I'm spending five out of seven nights at their place — but I guess I feel like if I'm going to be part of this, I have to be kind of solid with each of them. Hard to be balanced if you don't know what you're getting into.

Jamie and me, we talk about balance a lot. He says that it's not really about time spent with each person, but more about meeting needs. That kind of confused me until he pointed out that he likes playing ball, and Paul doesn't so much. "So, if it takes an hour and half to play one on one with me, and two hours to see a movie with Paul, does that mean you owe me a half hour? No."

Which makes sense, I guess.

Paul, on the other hand, is worried that all this getting to know them individually is already taking away from the whole. He's all, "I know you want to make sure you like us both, but you gotta know if we all work together, too." Which also makes sense. It's weird though, not knowing which is more important. If either is more important.

So we decide to do this for a while, but not think of it as a permanent thing. We'll spend time together in twos of course, just not in a regimented way. Not going to carve permanent dates into our schedules for all time.

Tonight I'm out with Paul. Well, I will be if Fred lets me take a long dinner break.

"You've been doing this a lot, Gent," he says, glaring at me. Fuck, he's big.

I nod, can't argue with that. "Yeah, but only on slow days and I don't go out for breaks or anything." I try to look cute and hopeful and not needed.

He snorts at me, his beard twitching, and I suspect he's just amused. "Paul's really getting to you," he teases.

I don't say anything — I mean, what would I say? 'Yeah, and his brother too'? I don't think so.

Finally, he sighs and looks over at Bobby, who just shakes his head and grins. "All right, get out of here. But be back by seven. And you can do the floors tonight."

I book. Not going to hang around when he could change his mind; not going to hang around when I can already see Paul walking up the street.

As soon as he's close enough to hear me over the noise of traffic I say hi and ask him how his day was. And just like that, we're in our own little world, holding hands as we walk to the diner on the corner. Not a real romantic place to eat, but it's close to work and we can sit in the back booth and talk.

Paul's had a good day despite the inherent internal politics of working at City Hall — and I get the feeling that office politics in a political building can get nasty. He tells me all the gossip as we wait for our food and I just let the names of unknown people float over me as I soak him in.

God, I've got it bad.

So, we eat and chat, and suddenly Paul asks me about my mom. "You talk about your dad sometimes, but never your mom. Did she pass away?"

Okay, I really should have seen that coming at some point, shouldn't I? I mean, people at least mention their parents, and with Paul and Jamie's folks gone, it's a natural question. Doesn't mean I want to answer, though.

I shake my head and pick up another French fry. "Not as far as I know," I say. "But then, I wouldn't know. She left when I was six."

Paul's eyes get really big and he looks at his plate. "Oh. Um. That sucks."

True enough. "Yeah. Dad says she couldn't stay anymore, that she had a lot bad things happen in her life and she couldn't deal with being a wife and mother and the basics of even taking care of herself. I guess she was depressed or something: Dad just said she was sick a lot. I remember her a little, but no matter how hard a I try I can't remember her ever smiling."

I remember her yelling. I remember her crying. I remember she always had a blue shirt on, and jeans. Sometimes her hair was tied back, but mostly it was down and sometimes it was tangled.

I remember the sound of her crying and not knowing why, except it had to be about me. I couldn't seem to draw her enough pictures, be quiet enough, stay out of the way enough. I remember getting my cereal and spilling it and being terrified.

I remember Dad telling me she'd gone away for a few days, and I remember asking him why she didn't come back.

I blink and realise Paul's looking at me again, his head tilted to the side. "You okay?"

"Yeah," I say, real fast. Too fast. I shrug. "Just haven't thought about it for a while. We did okay, you know?" That might be an exaggeration; I haven't spoken to my Dad in a long time, but Paul seems willing enough to accept it.

Or so I thought. You can never really tell with him, he backs away from stuff and then brings it back up when he's ready. This would be one of those times. We're walking back to the parlor after dinner and he says, "I find it really hard to understand, Gent."

I don't say anything, just nod and wait.

"My mom and dad, they were really good people, they loved us so much. I guess me and Jamie grew up a little sheltered — people in our lives got divorced, but I can't think of anyone who lost a parent like you did. I can't imagine what would be going on inside her head to leave a little boy. Her boy." He stops walking and looks me in the eye. "Can't imagine why she'd leave you."

I'm not the kind of guy who cries on the street. I haven't cried about my mother for years, and I'm not about to now.

"It wasn't about me," I say, because that's what I'm supposed to say. That's what I've been told, all my life; it wasn't my fault. "It was about her. I'm over it." It wasn't my fault. I am over it. I am.

Maybe someday it won't be a lie.

Out with Jamie, for lunch in the park. I have a couple of hours before work, he's got forty-five minutes. We've discovered that it's about the right time for us — half an hour and we're rushed, an hour and we're not talking, just making out.

"So," Jamie says around a mouthful of sandwich, "Paul told me about your mom."

Of course he did. I'm really starting to catch onto this thing; what one knows, they both know. That's good, generally. I mean, it's got to cut down on most misunderstandings, right? But it does tend to bring up sore spots more often than I'm used to. I sigh before I can stop myself. "Yeah."

"Heavy stuff, pretty boy." He's looking at me seriously, but somehow not intrusively. Like that's all he had to say, but he's willing to listen if I want to say more. It's good to know, but I really don't want to hash that shit out again.

"Not a pretty boy," I say with a growl, then wink at him.

He snorts and then coughs. Guess he shouldn't do that when he's swallowing. When he can breathe again he says, "Better fix your mirror, pretty. You're... very pretty."

I glare at him. "Girls are pretty."

"So are boys with your hair and features."

"Shut up."

"You shut up."

"That makes no sense."

"Doesn't have to. I'm the oldest."

I raise an eyebrow at him. "Are you?"

He nods and passes me his Coke. "Older than Paul by nine minutes, and a few hours older than you."

"Huh. Cool, I guess."

"So not only are you the pretty one, you're the baby." He looks terribly smug, the prick.

I drink from his Coke and think about that. Doesn't seem quite right, really. I shake my head and pass the can back to him. "Nope. Paul's the baby. Might be older, but trust me. He's my baby, your baby brother, and that's the way it is."

Jamie peers at me for a second and finishes the Coke, then lobs the can into a nearby bin. "Two points. And you might be right. What does that make me?"

I look him up and down and leer a little. "Hot."

"Yeah, yeah. Listen, got a book reading tomorrow night at the shop, wanna come? You and Paul can sit on the couch and look all cute together."

I laugh and shake my head. "Work. Bet Paul will go, though."

Jamie nods. "Yeah, I'll make him."

"Is that some perk of being the oldest — you can make us do what you want?"

"Yep." Jamie grins at me for a second and I grin back. Then he laughs a little, says, "Actually, Paul's the pushy one. He got us together, you know that?"

I shake my head. "I know nothing. Well, other than the two of you started up in a threesome, he told me that much."

Jamie stands up and starts to walk, waiting as I scramble to keep up. I guess we're going for a walk in the park.

"I came out when I was fourteen," Jamie says, his hands shoved in his pockets, which, trust me, I notice. I hold hands with Paul all the time, but Jamie and me, we keep a distance when we're in public. I don't like it much, but I can see the reason behind it. "Paul, obviously, was cool with it, and Mom and Dad adjusted well. Their first reaction was to ask if I was sure and then to tell me they loved me. Other than that, there wasn't any fireworks when I was around — I think Mom cried sometimes, though."

I shrug a shoulder. "My dad flipped when he found out," I offer. "But then, I didn't tell him so much as get caught, so I guess it figured."

"Ouch."

"Yeah."

"Anyway, by the time I was sixteen I was getting... well, I was sixteen. I wanted to date."

"You wanted to fuck."

"I wanted to fuck." He grins at me and I nod. I was a teenager, I know these things. "Didn't though. I was on so many teams and things I didn't have time, and I was pretty nervous about letting anyone really know I was into guys. You don't want to get caught alone in a locker room after practice, you know?"

Oh yeah, I know about that too.

"So, I never really went out much. Messed around a bit, but didn't really have anyone serious. Then the accident happened, and me and Paul were pretty useless for months. Went to school, came home, sat and stared at the walls. Our grandmother was living with us, so we were okay, but we were too messed up to... to be messing around."

I can see that. Don't know what it feels like, but I can picture it, picture them being lost and sad and alone.

"Just after we turned eighteen Paul started coming into my room at night. He had horrid nightmares, was even in therapy for them. Every night, he'd be shaking and screaming and crying... unless he slept with me. The doctor said he was relieving the trauma and needed to know that he still had family. I didn't care, I just wanted him better, and if he was sleeping in my bed that was fine with me. Wasn't supposed to be a lifetime thing; he'd get better as his subconscious figured out I was still alive, still loved him. The doctor said that so long as we were both comfortable with it, fine. Not good long term, but for a while..."

He looks at me, and I nod to let him know I get it. And I can see how that would sort of start things; teenagers, one messed up, the other hurting too — only natural to take comfort where you can find it.

"Paul never told our parents he's gay. Hell, he might not even be gay — we don't know. I know he liked girls fine when he was younger, but he was a book geek and shy and never really made any effort to date anyone, let alone guys." Jamie looks at me and smiles a little. "Paul was a late bloomer. Maybe he's gay, maybe he's bi... doesn't matter. Only thing that matters is how it turned out."

"Yeah," I say. "But I think he's definitely on the queer side. Nothing shy about the way he went after me."

Jamie considers that for a second. "Yeah, maybe you're right. Anyway, back then there wasn't anything going on. He'd wake up in the morning and tumble out of bed, and that was it. Then he started leaving earlier and earlier; I'd wake up and it'd still be dark, and his side of the bed was cold. I'd look for him sometimes, and find him up and dressed at five-thirty. Or watching TV. I knew he wasn't sleeping well and I kind of freaked a little, thought the nightmares were getting worse and that he'd make himself sick."

We walk a little way in silence. I'm kind of watching him, but he seems okay, just lost in thought. We turn a corner in the path, start heading back toward his store. "So what happened?" I ask finally.

Jamie blinks and looks at me, then grins. "Sorry. Um, he... he had this friend. I was after Paul all the time, telling him he had to talk to me, that I was worried, that I wanted him to sleep in my bed, that I was cool with it. Part I wasn't telling him was that I really missed him when I woke up, that I was having a pretty major mental fit over how much I wanted him there. God, first time I woke up wrapped up in him I got hard in, like, three seconds." He shrugs. "I liked it. Knew it was wrong, but I liked it anyway."

"And he was... what? Flipped about it?"

"Nah, he didn't know. Turns out he was freaking about the same thing, spending all his time away from the house talking to this guy about it or jerking off in the shower. He wanted me, he had to talk it out."

Right, so I'm not stupid. I'm also starting to think I'm never ever going to know the name of their ex-lover. Whatever — it's not important to me. But it's one more weird thing on top of the pile.

"Okay. So... you guys obviously figured something out," I say.

Jamie tilts his head and flashes me another grin, the one that Paul never manages to pull off. It's wicked and dirty and I just freaking love it. Almost as much as the slow shy one Paul has that Jamie can't do.

"Not really," Jamie says, then dances away when I try to smack him. He seems to really like making me work for information he's actually offering for free — it's just on his terms, which is really something I should think about later. Control issues, maybe; not that that's a bad thing, if channelled in the right direction. However, it's not time to start thinking about Jamie topping me, it's time to listen and the man is talking.

"I wasn't talking about it. Paul wasn't talking to me. So the three of us got stinking drunk one night and it was forced out of us, both of us goaded into yelling and screaming and finally just saying it. I wanted us to go to Paul's therapist — I kinda figured we were just displacing stuff, working emotional shit out through our bodies. Being that age — we were nineteen by then — it seemed like every conceivable issue was manifesting through sex. I mean, Paul was having body issues, which made me freak 'cause he looks just like me and I thought we were fine, and then me wanting to sleep with him, and wanting to have sex with him... it just struck me as somewhat less than healthy."

No shit. Mind, I shouldn't listen to my voices — I am, after all, sleeping with both of them. Often. Together. I have my own issues. So I just nod and gently steer him off the path, to a bench near the gate. He doesn't seem to notice, and he sits facing me.

"Paul wouldn't. He spouted the same stuff back at me, said he knew it was fucked up, but he just wanted one single thing in his life that felt good, one person he knew he could count on. He asked me to trust him, to just give him a picture of what it was like to be loved for who he was, by someone who knew him inside and out and loved him anyway.

"And then he kissed me."

"Game over," I say quietly. I feel odd, sort of like I've been given a gift I didn't know I wanted until I had it. My stomach is a little light and I don't know what to say, how to tell Jamie thank you for letting me know this.

"Game over," he whispers back, meeting my eye. "That's all it took — not the kiss, but telling me what he needed, letting me know what he was prepared to deal with to be with me. We didn't go into this blind, Gent. There was a lot of shit after that, but there were some amazing times in the next three years. We were... really good together, for a long time."

"You miss it," I say, beginning to clue in.

He nods. "I do. Paul does. But that's not why we're with you — don't think you're a replacement. Paul and I, we need balance. We need a third, a buffer, someone to keep us in the world, to keep life real." He stands up and waits for me again, then leans in really close to talk in my ear. "We're not going to settle for just anyone, pretty. We're looking for a partner, not a quick lay." Then he kisses my cheek and steps back, like he's not said or done anything. "See you after work," he says softly.

"See ya," I agree, and then he turns and walks away, back to his shop. Oddly, I find the entire conversation reassuring. There was a time that getting into the heavy, important parts of a relationship would send me running, but this time... it makes me feel reassured that there's a point to this, that it's beyond sex and hanging out.

I think I like that.

Chapter Six

I've been cleaning my apartment all day, and I've barely got my hair dry and tied back when there's a knock on the door. It's the first time I've spent my day off like this and I'm not sure I like it. Before the twins I'd spend my day off sleeping, going downtown for a bit, shooting pool. Lately I've spent my time watching Jamie play ball or meeting Paul for lunch—generally just hanging out with them. Today? I clean my apartment and cook dinner. Shocking.

All right, it's a one time only event, and it's for a good cause. The three of us have been easing off on the dating thing a bit—which is good, it wasn't supposed to go on forever. I suspect that this will be the last 'date' I have with Paul for a while, and I sort of want it to be a good one; I even got him a present. He's never seen my place, so it's all tidy in its own substandard way, and I made pasta.

I let Paul in and he greets me with the shy smile and a kiss that's anything but. I may be mildly addicted to his contradictions. Anyway, he's here and I show him into the living room—by letting him take two steps forward from the door—and he looks around, one hand tangling with mine.

I feel a little self-conscious, a little embarrassed. I know it's dumb, but when I compare my place with theirs... well, it's not good. I live in a not so great area, have a tiny little over-priced one bedroom hovel that hasn't been redecorated since 1976. It's a far cry from their place, but Paul doesn't seem to care, which is nice. He's much more interested in the books on the shelves than the shelves themselves.

We talk about his day and spend twenty minutes or so poking through art books left over from when I was taking classes, and he looks around the rest of the place while I finish getting supper ready. Doesn't take long—the kitchen is open to the living room, there's one bedroom, a bathroom, and a closet. That's it.

Kindly, he doesn't make up nice things to say. "Your tub is blue," he says as we sit down to dinner. "This frightens me."

We're eating in the living room, sprawled on the couch. There's nothing wrong with the table, it's just us—we don't use the table at their place, either.

"Yeah. Well, aqua. At least it matches the sink." I wink at him and we spend a weird few minutes trying to figure out the designers of the 70's. Finally we just conclude that they were all on drugs, which also neatly explains polyester pants and the whole orange and brown color combination. It's a miracle my stove is white instead of olive.

We talk about cooking, debating gas ranges over electric—it's a fast conversation since neither of us has used gas—and then we do the dishes. I'd leave them, but God knows when I'll be back long enough to get them washed before gross stuff grows on them. It should scare the hell out of me, the amount of time I'm spending at their place, but it doesn't. Not really.

"Want to watch a movie?" I ask, steering him not so subtly back to the couch. I even have one rented, just in case he says yes.

"Sure," he says, but he's not looking toward my ancient TV, and he's not interested in any movie. He gives me a shove and I land on the couch, laughing. When he follows me down I flip him over and tickle him until he squirms, both of us laughing and trading kisses.

The tickling dies off and I settle for just kissing him, rubbing my hands all over his body. He's a little tiny bit slimmer than Jamie, not as defined. I'm way smaller than both of them, and I like that they're more substantial than me. I'm thinking about that as I make my way up his neck with my mouth, my fingers feeling his nipple rings through his shirt.

He groans and arches his neck.

"Like that?" I ask, not really needing him to answer. I think I ask him that every time I get to concentrate on his rings. He always answers the same too; it's becoming our thing. Jamie says it's cute, but it makes him roll his eyes at us.

"Yeah, harder," Paul says, right on cue.

I push his shirt up and there's a couple moments of uncoordinated struggle as he half sits up to pull it off and I dive for his chest. Soon enough, though, we're as comfortable as we can get, sprawled on the couch half-dressed. I go to town on his right nipple, licking and sucking and pulling on the ring with my teeth. He's moaning, holding my head in place and undoing my hair tie.

He likes to feel my hair over him when we make out. I hate that it gets in my mouth, but it really sends him wild, so I let it go. A worked up Paul is a happy Gent, and I don't look my gift horses in the mouth.

I pull at his other ring with my fingers and he bucks under me, rubbing his cock on me. I'm lying on top of him, between his legs, and fuck, he's hard. I am too, but feeling him drill into my belly like that is something else. He's gasping my name and his fingers are tangled in my hair, and he's about to pop.

So I have to decide if I want to make him come in his pants or if I want to play with the gift I got him. Easy choice.

He glares at me as I sit up, and I grin down at him, strip off my own shirt. I move my legs, straddle him and push my dick against his, just two layers of denim between us. Well, maybe a pair of shorts too, I don't know—all I know is I'm commando, and it wouldn't surprise me if he is, too.

We are so easy. The whole bunch of us.

"You look like you have something planned," he says, rocking against me.

"Do I?" I ask, trying to look sweet and innocent.

He rolls his eyes at me, the brat. "Yeah. But if it involves less clothes than this, I'm in."

I grin and bend down to kiss him; he tastes like marinara sauce and red wine. When I let him go we're both a little breathless again and he's looking kind of dazed. When I try to stand up, he pouts.

"Shush, baby. Got something for you." I climb off and go to my bag, already packed by the door.

"Rubbers?" he says hopefully. "Flavoured lube?"

"Better," I promise, taking the small package to him. "But yeah, got rubbers and lube too, not flavoured though."

"Good, they never taste like what they're supposed to be." He sits up and reaches for the package, smiling up at me. I hold it back and swat his hand away. "Hey!" he protests, laughing. "Thought it was for me?"

"It is," I assure him. "But first you gotta take off your pants."

He stares at me for a moment and then laughs. "That line usually work for you?" he asks. But he stands up and undoes his jeans, toeing off his shoes at the same time.

"Yup," I grin at him. Then I strip off too, both of us grinning like fools. Both of us naked and hard under our jeans.

"We're so easy," he says ruefully.

"Lie down," I tell him, one hand holding the present, the other digging in my jeans for a rubber.

He does as he's told, pulling idly at his dick. "Going to fuck me?" he asks, spreading his legs.

"Nope." I grab the lube from behind the couch and toss it to him. "You're going to do me."

His cock jumps and mine gives a sympathetic twitch. "Whatever you say," Paul agrees happily.

In short order I'm straddling him again, his fingers in my ass as I roll the rubber over his prick and stroke him a bit. "Gent." He shudders when he says my name. "Go easy or this is gonna end."

I nod, wiggle down on his fingers a bit. "S'okay, baby. I'm ready."

He looks at me for a long moment and jabs his fingers in deep, twisting a bit. Makes me cry out, and then he grins. "Yeah, okay. Climb on."

I laugh and gasp at the same time, lift my hips up so I can get in the right place. I sink onto him, not as smooth as I'd like, but it's been a while since I've bottomed from the top, so to speak. He's good to me though, doesn't move until I'm all the way down on him, and then he just shimmies his hips a little, enough to make us both groan.

"Okay, now wait a sec," I say, holding up the gift I got

him.

He nods, hands on my hips, eyes on the prize.

"Paul. Stop looking at my cock."

"No."

I sigh and tug on his nipples.

"Jesus!" He bucks up and we both freeze, panting.

"Don't do that!" I tell him.

"Then don't do that!" he says back.

When we can both breathe without fear of shooting, I wave the parcel in front of his face. "Now, this isn't the best there is, baby, but it's a start. Hope it drives you nuts."

He pries his hands off my hips and takes the present from me, looking me in the eye. "Sure it will. It's from you, yeah?"

"I drive you nuts?"

"Only in the best possible way, of course."

"Of course. Open it."

He rips the paper off and looks at the plastic bag, turning it a little. He makes an appreciative noise and shimmies again. "This what I think it is?"

"Uh huh."

"Put it on me." That's possibly the first time I've heard Paul give an order. It's certainly the first time I've heard that tone of voice, and my hands need no help from my brain before they're reaching out and dumping the silver chain onto his stomach.

It's a light chain, nothing fancy. It's smoother than mine, has a bit more style, but it's nothing like what I want to see on him. It's got clasps at both ends so it can come off easily, and it only takes about three seconds before I have it on his left nipple. I pull it gently and his eyes roll.

"Gent."

I chuckle and attach it to the right as well, then start

to play. I have every intention of making him crazy, of torturing him until he fucks me hard, and I get off to a good start. His hands fly back to my hips and his eyes close tight, curses flowing from his mouth as he gasps and moans.

There is, however, one little flaw in my plan, and I don't see it until his eyes fly open and I see the devil in him. I barely have time to squeak before he lets go of my hips and nimble fingers tug at my own chain, dangling so invitingly in front of him.

From then on it's kind of a blur. There's swearing from both of us, a series of sounds that mean "Oh God, yes!" and my yelling for him to fuck me. We're grinding and thrusting and I've got his chain in one hand and my cock in the other and he's begging for me to stop or do it harder and for me to come. I don't think I can wait for him.

He's huge in my ass, pounding up as I slam down and every twitch of my nipple chain is sending jolts to my cock and ass and I can just feel it everywhere. He's arching off the couch, and I'm tugging at his chain, and I know he's feeling it too.

"Jesus, Gent," he whispers. "Just come for me. Come on me, wanna see you shoot, want it to hit my face—"

I lose it. Just fucking lose it, my dick spasming and come flying out of me, scorching trails on his chest and neck, and there's a line of it across his mouth. He licks his lips and I can feel his cock throb in my ass, feel him come in me.

He's beautiful in silver chains.

Eventually we come down a bit and take a shower. We're both a little loopy, so we have the rest of the wine I used in the sauce, and when my hair is dry I call for a cab.

It's not too late, only about ten-thirty or so, which means Jamie should still be awake if we're lucky.

On the way out of the building I remember I haven't checked my mail in about a week, so I grab it from the mailbox as the cab pulls up and stuff it in my bag. There's not a lot, just my cable bill and a bunch of junk from the bank, a couple of magazines. No pink envelopes, which is nice—means my heat stays on for a while longer.

We get to the apartment and find Jamie watching a ballgame on TV, cursing the uselessness of the other team. I don't even know what sport's on. Neither does he when Paul stands in front of him and takes off his shirt.

Jamie's eyes go wide and then he grins at me. "Nice."

I grin back. "Thanks. Baby wore me out. He really likes it."

Jamie laughs and grabs Paul, hauls him down onto his lap. "Good to know. You shouldn't break Gent, though. It's not nice."

Paul snorts. "Was so nice."

Jamie tugs at the chain and Paul goes still. I smile and reach for my bag, toss Jamie lube and a rubber.

"Not up for playing?" Jamie asks, one eyebrow up.

"I'm up," I tell him. "Well, almost. Just like watching." And I do. Really really. Sometimes it's just nice to watch and stroke off.

So that's what we do, right there in the living room. I watch Jamie fuck Paul from behind, watch that chain catch the light, and I pull on my dick, remember what it felt like earlier. My ass is sore, but every time Jamie makes Paul's breath catch I can feel my hole spasm. It's like an orgasm that doesn't stop, and soon enough I'm tugging at my own nipples, legs spread as I jerk off over them. I come on Jamie's back, watch Paul shoot through Jamie's fingers. Jamie fucking howls as he comes.

Not bad for a day off, really.

We clean up the mess and head to bed, Paul scooping up my bag as he passes it, then swears as the mail slides out, all over the place.

"No trouble," I tell him, and I bend down to gather it up. Two magazines, a flyer for the supermarket, the bank statements, a letter from the company that owns my building, and the cable bill. I toss it all back in the bag except for the realty thing, which I open and read as I walk.

"Ah fuck." My building is going condo and I have a month to let them know if I'll be buying my apartment or moving out. Lovely.

"What's up?" Jamie asks, coming in from the bathroom. He's damp from a fast shower, but at least he doesn't reek of sex anymore. Hard to sleep next to a man that smells of spunk.

"Gotta move," I tell him, and I give him the letter as I strip off for bed. Paul's already in, way over on his side. I slide in next to him and give him another kiss.

Jamie gets in, but he's got his thinking face on. He kisses me and leans over to kiss Paul good night, then we all settle in and the boys turn off the lights. There's a heavy silence, which is really hard to fall asleep in.

"What?" I finally say into the dark.

Jamie's light snaps on. "Move in here."

I blink. "What?"

Paul's light comes on. "That would work," he says.

"What?" I say again. "It's a little soon, isn't it?"

Jamie and Paul both shrug. Jamie says, "You're here almost every night."

Paul says, "Why pay rent on a place you're never at?"

I say, "But—"

And then Jamie looks at me, his face serious. "It's up to you, Gent. But you can live here if you want. If it'll make you feel better, you can even pay rent, say a hundred dollars less than your old place 'cause you'll have more transportation costs. A third of utilities."

Every relationship eventually reaches a stage where you have to make a choice. Is this long term? Is it something you're prepared to take a real risk for? Is this the time to finally just give yourself over and make the decision that this is something you want and are willing to work for? Could this maybe turn into love?

And I've just reached that point. Suddenly, without knowing it, I've found myself at the point where I have to either walk away from them or give them everything.

It doesn't take me that long to know what I want. I look at Jamie and then I look at Paul and I just know. "Okay."

Chapter Seven

I'm laughing my ass off, watching Fred and Bobby try to get my couch into the parlor. I mean, it's nice that they bought it and all, and it'll be nice to have a comfy place to sit... but it's hysterically funny watching two huge biker guys fight with a couch. They've tried it on its side, on one end, with the cushions off—and now they're just kind of looking at it like it'll get itself into the parlor by its own power.

Paul's just standing on the curb, chewing on the inside of his lip. I know he knows how to make it work, but he's scared of Fred. I told him that Fred's a big softy, but sometimes Paul gets an idea and won't let go of it. Apparently six foot four and damn close to three hundred pounds with a thick beard and a vat of ink on his arms equals scary in Paul's world.

Okay, Fred used to scare the hell out of me too.

I go over to Paul and sort of lean into him. "Want to tell me, and I'll tell them?"

I thought I asked nice and low, but Bobby spins around and looks at me. "Somethin' to say, smartass?"

Paul sort of shrinks a little and I brush his arm with mine. "He means me," I say, and Bobby laughs.

"Yeah, you're not a smartass, Paul. Not very bright, letting this one move in with you, but not a smartass." He grins maniacally and I wince.

"Tone it down, Bobby," I say mildly.

"Or what?" he asks as a tease. Fred's watching us, leaning on the door frame and looking utterly unimpressed.

"Or I'll tell Paul we can go now and he won't tell you how to get the damn couch in the building," I say smugly.

"And how are you gonna get your boxes over to his place?" Bobby says, pointing to the van which contains most of my stuff. His van.

"Like this." I reach into my pocket and pull out his keys. Then I run like hell, Fred laughing and Bobby yelling behind me. I almost get around the block before I figure out Bobby's not chasing me anymore, but I still take my time walking back. I may be a fool, but I'm not stupid.

I'm almost back to the parlor when I realise that all I can see of the couch is the last foot or so, braced up by Fred, and then he shoves and it's in. Paul's standing to the side looking pleased with himself.

"Was just angles and leverage," he says when I walk up.

I nod, trying not to look winded.

"Asshole," Bobby says as he comes out and swats me on the head. "Keys?"

I grin and hand them over as Fred shakes Paul's hand and thanks him. Fred's hand is huge, swallowing up Paul's, but they seem to have reached a new level—Paul doesn't look at all terrified anymore, although he's deeply suspicious of Bobby.

"Wish you hadn't let him shove a needle through your

nipples?" I whisper at him.

Paul blushes and looks at his shoes.

God he's cute.

"So that's it?" Bobby asks as he puts down the last of the boxes. "Not much, Gent. You've been living in a closet?"

He laughs; I roll my eyes.

"Sold a lot," I tell him when he gasps out the last giggle. That's an understatement, really. I sold everything I could. Fred bought the couch, the girl who lived above me bought everything in my kitchen, some guy took the bed. I sold the TV, the VCR, the stereo... just about all I'm bringing with me is clothes and books, a lot of art. Lots of pencils and stuff like that, and pictures. I guess it doesn't look like much, piled on the sidewalk outside the apartment building.

Fred offers to park the van somewhere and help us haul it all upstairs, but Paul and I figure that if we put it in the elevator we can do it one trip, so we all just grab a couple of boxes and that's it. Going up in the world.

I think Fred thinks so too, the way he's assessing the building. He looks faintly surprised, and a little uncomfortable. I make a mental note to tell him that Paul inherited the apartment, that he's not some rich kid—thought why that would bother Fred is beyond me. Why it would bother me that Fred would think that is a little confusing too.

So I do the smart thing and wave goodbye, promise to be at work tomorrow, and close the door on them.

The ride up is too short to do more than sneak a kiss—we've tried for more before, but testing has conclusively proven that there's no way to get more than a quick feel in. Doesn't hurt to prove it again, though.

When we reach our floor Paul presses the hold button and we push and shove the boxes into the hall as fast as we can, then let the elevator go. I'm just standing in front of all my shit, looking down the hall to the front door. "Think Jamie will help?"

"He better," Paul grumbles. "Proud enough of those muscles—and besides, we want to watch him work, don't we?"

Oh hell yeah.

We grab a couple of boxes and take them in, using one to prop the door open so we can just go in and out, call out for Jamie and head back for the rest. Two trips later he's not come out and we're mostly done.

Paul frowns at the pile of boxes and goes to stand in front of the big window, peering out. "His bike's here," he says, then calls Jamie's name again.

I shrug. "He'll turn up, baby." I go over and put my arms around him, my hands on him, and kiss him nice and slow. He melts into me, and we're just kind of lost in it, the feel of kissing, of being home.

Until a throat being cleared behind us makes Paul pull away. I turn around and Jamie's standing there looking embarrassed, and some old guy in a suit is next to him.

"Um, William's here, Paul," Jamie says, his voice all apologetic.

Paul just stands there, his mouth open.

William—whoever the hell he is—clears his throat again. "I'm sorry, Paul. I didn't mean to intrude." Then he looks at me and sort of smiles. "You must be the gentleman Jamie's been telling me about. Although he left out a few details."

We all sort of make inarticulate noises, and I think Paul might choke, but he seems to snap out of it, literally shaking it off like he's a wet Lab or something.

"William, this is Gent. Gentleman. Don't make a joke, he doesn't like it."

William nods, though I'm not sure if it's for the warning or in acknowledgement of the introduction.

Paul holds onto my arm, almost like he's staking a claim—which I so don't mind—and says, "Gent, this is William Gorman, our lawyer. Well, Dad's lawyer, then our lawyer, and more of a family friend than anything else."

Lovely.

"Nice to meet you," I say and give him a nod of my own. Then we all stand there looking at each other.

"What brings you by?" Paul finally asks.

William shrugs one elegant shoulder and I hate him a little bit. "It's been a while, I thought I'd stop in and see how you were. Jamie was rearranging things in your father's office and told me you were getting a roommate. We were discussing... financial matters when you got here." He looks a little embarrassed. "I'm afraid I assumed you were taking on a roommate because you needed money. Jamie didn't see fit to set me right about the situation." He give Jamie a faintly accusing look, which is neatly deflected by a shrug.

"Not my tale to tell, is it?" he says, ironically. "Paul's a big boy, over the age of consent, and Gent's a great guy."

Jesus fuck I want to go over there and kiss him. Want to tell the whole damn world that Jamie is a great guy, that he's a damn fine lover... but the secret keeps us all safe, lets us be together.

I just wish the pain could be shared around a little, would have been happy to let this lawyer guy thing I was with Jamie, let Fred and Bobby think I'm with Paul. But no, he had to walk in when I was shoving my tongue down Paul's throat.

Jamie smiles at me, and I can see the parts of it that don't reach his eyes. Paul's fingers, digging into my arm, tell me the same thing.

I realise we've been quiet for a while and I'm probably just in the way of some family kind of thing, so I disengage from Paul as gently as I can. "Going to go put some stuff away," I say softly. "Let you talk." And I kiss him again, just once, because I have to. He's pale and he looks like he's about to fall over.

Before I leave the room with a box under my arm Jamie is by Paul's side and his arms are crossed. The Wall of Twins has been formed, and I doubt William fucking Gorman stands a chance.

I get my books out and on the shelves Jamie cleared for me, and then go for another box and then another. The three of them are sitting on the couch and from little bits I overhear as I pass by William is apologizing for everything under the sun—for showing up unannounced, for not paying enough attention to know that Paul's gay, for just being out of touch for too long.

Paul seems rather unimpressed that William didn't know he's gay, but Jamie thinks it's funny.

"Not like you advertise it," Jamie says. I decide to stay in the kitchen for a moment or two. Okay, I so shouldn't be eavesdropping, but hell—not like it really matters at this point. The man's a lawyer, he probably expects me to.

So I grab a box and put it on the table and try to quietly peel the tape off while I listen in.

"Like you do?" Paul says back, all snotty.

William laughs. "Well, yeah. More than you, anyway."

Someone chokes, I think it's Jamie. "What do you mean?" Yeah, Jamie, and he sounds amused and pissy at the same time.

William clears his throat. "Well, you used to spend an awful lot of time looking at Carl's butt at the office."

There's a short silence and Paul bursts out laughing. "Carl? You're serious? Man, I had no idea Carl was your type. What with him being, like, fifty."

"He was thirty-four," Jamie protests and there's dead silence.

"Um. You didn't..." William finally says. "Because legally—"

"God, no. He had a nice ass," Jamie says. "But he also had a wife and a girlfriend—unless you didn't know that, in which case let's just say he's straight and move on, okay? I need water. Back in a minute."

Before I can really do more than pick up the box and head to the hallway Jamie flies in.

"Man, this is weird," he whispers to me. And then he's kissing me, shoving his tongue into my mouth and pulling away again. "I wanna fuck you. Right now, I wanna fuck you with him here, want to do it real fast? Bathroom?"

"Jesus Christ," I gasp out. "Are you crazy?"

"Maybe. Yeah, I guess so. But it's wild and I'm flying and Paul's freaked and he just won't go—too busy making up for... everything."

Jamie's almost shaking, and he's grinning like mad, but there's something kind of frantic in his eyes that worries me. I put the box down and push him into the fridge with my body, pin him there. I can feel his heart race.

"Hey, calm down a bit," I say softly. "It'll be okay, he'll go and you and Paul can be hysterical. It's all right, Jamie—really."

He nods and takes a deep breath, tilts his head back on the fridge. "I can hear them talking still," he whispers.

"Their voices."

I kiss his neck and rub at his back, his arms; it's weird, but I can feel him start to come down a bit. And go up a lot, poking into me.

"Adrenaline junkie," I tease.

"You know it," he says back.

"I thought Paul would be the one freaking," I whisper. "Listen for them."

And it's way more stupid than the bathroom, so far beyond crazy that it scares me a bit, but I reach down and start jacking him through his sweatpants, rubbing at this dick and balls and basically letting him hump me.

He's panting and I'm working him, his hips are twisting and bucking, and he slams his hand on mine and just grinds, his eyes closed tight and his mouth open. I stare at him as he comes, feel his cock move under my hand and feel the wet stain spread. He sort of groans and I step back, shaking.

"Um, which room," I hiss at him, holding my box and willing him to just stand up and stop looking newly fucked. Oh my God, I can't believe I just did that, that we were so stupid.

He blinks and me and shakes his head, then goes to the sink and splashes some water on his face. He dries off really fast and grabs a box, holds it in front of him— and damn, if he suddenly looks less like a slut. Wild. The amazing transforming Jamie.

"What's in these boxes?" he asks me, and I look at him really closely.

He looks calmer, the wild spark gone, and I can't tell if there's anything wrong anymore. Maybe I'll look into the adrenaline thing.

"Clothes and pictures in that one, more art supplies in this one," I tell him. "There's only a couple of boxes left, and they're mostly clothes."

He nods and walks down the hall in front of me. "Put the art supplies in Dad's study for now," he whispers. "We'll shift them after Paul's old room is empty for you. Clothes and stuff, obviously, go in here." He opens the door at the end, which I'd thought of as the guest room, and sends me in. "Home sweet home. Until William blows off, anyway."

I snort and toss the box on the bed. It really does look like a guestroom—I hope William doesn't look in, no way does Paul sleep in here.

Jamie takes off to change and I lug the rest of the boxes into their temporary rooms. By the time I'm done Paul and Jamie are gently ushering William to the door.

"Well, Gent. It's been... interesting meeting you," he says, and then he gives me this grin, like he's in on a wonderful, happy secret and suddenly I like him. He loves my boys. He's been cool about Jamie being gay and he's cool with Paul.

I smile at him and nod. "It's been good," I say.

He turns to the boys and hugs them each, makes them promise to call soon. We'll all go out for dinner, he says. And talk about books and art and real estate and what's wrong with big business.

Jamie snorts and insists that sports get some air time and Paul comes over to me and takes my hand, that shy smile on his face again.

Not a bad day, really. Paul came out, Jamie got off, I got a new home. Feels good to be me.

Chapter Eight

Bobby and Fred are waiting for me when I get to work, and I can tell that it's bad news. They're sitting in the main room and it's quiet, and that's just not the way the place is. Usually you can barely hear yourself think in there, the music is so loud, even when we're not open.

I go and sit down and look at them. "What?"

Fred leans back in his chair and looks at the ceiling. "We're making them re-check, Gent. Don't get me wrong, I'm sure it's a fuck up at the lab. But until they call back and give me the all clear you got time off."

I think I'm gonna pass out.

"What did I test out on?"

He doesn't answer for a long time and all I'm thinking is how many fucking high risk groups I'm in. Gay. More than one guy. Work with needles. Spend my time wiping fucking blood off people. Oh shit, what if I gave something to my boys? "What the fuck did I test positive for?" I think I'm screaming.

He tells me he doesn't know, that he just gets the word

that employee number whatever had a contaminated or infected sample and can't work until retesting is done and said employee is proven clean.

I go home.

I just sit in the living room for a bit, trying to remember if I *ever* stuck myself with the needle when I was doing a tattoo. If even once I had a torn glove. Hell, half the time I wear two gloves on each hand. Clients don't have to prove they're clean, so we have to make sure that we're safe and clean and follow all the regs and fucking take care of ourselves.

I think I might lose it sitting there. All I can think about is when the hell did I fuck up? How did it happen without me noticing? I'm meticulous about my hands, I check for cuts and scrapes all the time. I just can't remember. Maybe it didn't happen. Maybe the fucking lab got a false positive. That happens, right?

My boys. Fuck. If I gave them anything I'll never forgive myself. The way we are, one gets it the other one will too, even if they don't touch me ever again. And they may not.

That thought sends me to the bedroom and I start throwing my shit in a bag. Not gonna let my boys get sick. Not gonna hurt my twins. Not gonna let them get sick.

I stop when I realize that leaving now isn't going to change a fucking single thing. If I passed it on then it's done, and the least I can do is stick around to pay for it. To help. If they let me. Besides, where the hell would I go? This is home.

God, I can't think. I go to the kitchen and grab the phone, call Fred. I gotta yell so he can hear me over the music.

"When will they call? Will they call me or you?"

He turns off the racket, or closes a door or something.

"They'll call me to tell me if you can work or not. They'll call you with the results and talk to you about it."

"When? Why the hell hasn't anyone called me about this?"

"They said they would. Check your machine, Gent."

I look down and see the blinking light. "'kay. Sorry. When will they get back to us?"

"First they're going to go back and trace the numbers. Make sure that the vials were really your blood, you know? If it was, they'll re-test. You'll probably have to go back in and get another needle. Look, man. Listen to me. They fucked up. I know it, you know it. No fucking way you got anything off these needles, you're too careful."

I just nod, then realize I'm on the phone. "Yeah." My voice sounds hollow.

He doesn't say anything for a moment. "Paul. He's gonna be okay with this. He'll take care of you until this shit is cleared up."

I nod again. They don't know about Jamie. "Yeah, he'll be cool. Listen, I gotta go. Call if you hear anything."

I hang up the phone, delete the message and head out to the Razor's Edge. It's one in the afternoon.

They find me there at ten-thirty. I've had more to drink than I can ever remember and I'm still sitting there, having another beer. I feel fine.

Paul slides in next to me in the booth and Jamie across, and they just look at me. I try to grin, but it doesn't really make it past being just a thought.

"You ready to come home?" Paul asks.

I sort of nod and Jamie's just… he's just staring at me. Then he stands up and Paul stands up and I think about standing up.

"Fuck." I think I say it out loud, but maybe I don't.

Jamie and Paul look at each other. They reach over and haul me up and I find out I can walk. Well, in fact.

Chris Owen

We leave the bar and start walking, keeping an eye out for a cab.

"How long you been there?" Jamie asks.

"Before two. What time is it now?" I see a cab and point, let Paul do the flagging down.

"Almost eleven. What happened?"

Jamie won't look at me. He's beyond pissed. I don't know why. If he doesn't know what happened why is he mad at me? Not like I made him come looking for me.

Paul's pulling on my arm, getting me to climb into the cab. I get in, Paul's in back with me. Jamie goes around and sits in front.

Paul's looking at me with wide eyes. "You didn't work today. We saw your stuff on the bed and called the shop. They said you took the day off and I should go find you. Fred's pissed."

Oh crap.

I lean my head back on the car seat. "Tell you about it when we get home, 'kay?"

Paul nods and looks out his window. His hands are in his lap, tight fists, and his mouth is down at the corners. I'm scaring him.

I hate this.

We get home and go into the living room. Jamie is practically vibrating. Paul's... well, Paul's quiet. My bag is on the couch, the shit I packed still in it. But nothing else. They didn't help me along, anyway.

Paul sits on the couch and looks at me. I sit down in the easy chair and try to figure out what to say. I look at Jamie. He's staring at me, eyes hard. He moves to stand behind Paul, one hand on his twin's shoulder.

Right. Them. Me. Got it.

It's Paul who finally asks. "What happened between getting up and going to work, Gent?"

I look down at the floor and back up at them, run a

hand through my hair. My hair is fucking everywhere, not sure when I lost the elastic.

"Went to work. Had to leave." I look at them and they don't get it. I gotta open my mouth, tell my boys what I've done to them. And Christ, I didn't know that anything could hurt like this.

"I... I got a positive test."

Paul's off the couch and on me before I can blink, holding me and telling me it's gonna be okay. He's shaking. I gather him up and start talking, tell him I'm always so careful at work, that I can't remember being stuck, that I'm sure the lab made a mistake and oh God, Paul I'm so sorry. I'm so sorry. I'm so sorry.

He's listening. He's nodding his head. He's telling me that I'm right, that the lab made a mistake, that he knows how careful I am. He's telling me that the lab will call back and it will all be okay.

We sit there for a bit and then Jamie clears his throat. I reach out, ready to pull him in so I can tell him how scared I am, how sorry I am that I've done this horrible thing to him and Paul.

But he's not there. He's still standing behind the couch.

"You were gonna leave."

I look at him and Paul slides off my lap and sits on the floor at my feet.

"I wasn't thinking, Jamie. Was gonna go before I made you sick. But it could already be too late." I look at my bag. Jamie's looking at me and he's still mad. "Jamie, I'm sorry. I just wanted to save you from—"

"Who did you think it was?" His eyes. Oh fuck, his eyes are hard and I don't understand.

"I told you, I don't remember anything. Can't remember getting stuck, can't remember cuts or scrapes—"

"Jamie thinks you figured one of us was screwing

around," Paul says real quietly.

Everything stops. Jamie looks at me and I can't tell what he's thinking. One of them? One of my boys cheating? The thought hadn't crossed my mind. Until now. And because I'm scared and drunk and hurt and for a million other bad reasons I say, "Guilty conscience, Jamie?"

"Fuck you." He turns and leaves, goes to the bedroom. Paul goes after him.

I stay where I am.

I can hear them. I can hear them yelling, Jamie swearing and Paul telling him to calm down. Paul's telling him that I didn't mean it, that before Jamie said it I hadn't even thought of it. Jamie says something about not even knowing what the positive was for and I remember the message on the machine. I don't know either.

It goes on for ages. I can hear them talking quietly for a long time. I fall asleep in the chair.

It feels really late when I wake up. It's still dark, and the lights are all off except the one on the side table, next to the couch. My bag is gone. I try to sit up, but I feel sick, so I stay where I am.

Then there are arms lifting me, carrying me to the couch, and I can lie down. A cool hand pushes my hair off my face and I try to open my eyes, but I can't. I whisper "Thanks," and go back to sleep.

The next time I wake up it's almost morning. Jamie is sitting on the couch beside me, brushing my hair. He's not making any noise, but his face is wet.

"I'm sorry," I whisper. "I never thought that. I didn't, Jamie. It's my fault. I'm so sorry."

He shakes his head and says, "No. Not your fault. Nothing is wrong with you. There can't be, we just found you, see? I'm sorry. I'm scared and I thought you were walking out on us too, and I just didn't think and I'm so sorry, Gent."

I push myself up. "Not walking. Not running. Just... just please, Jamie. Tell me you know that I trust you."

He nods and leans forward, his forehead on mine. "I know it. I really do. I'm so sorry I was such a bastard."

I close my eyes and take a deep breath. "We okay?"

He kisses me really softly. "We're okay. And you are, too. You have to be."

We sit there while the sun comes up, Jamie brushing my hair and me trying not to think.

Paul comes out of the bedroom at seven thirty. He looks at us and comes over, kisses us both good morning and sits down on the floor.

"Gent?"

"Yeah, baby?"

"What was the positive for?" He's looking like it damn near broke him to ask. Christ how anyone managed to sleep last night...

I shake my head. "Don't know. I deleted the message on the machine."

They stare at me.

"Okay," Jamie finally says. "Do you want to go retrieve it, or should one of us?"

I look at them and see that there's no way they're gonna let me pretend that this isn't happening. I stand up and go to the kitchen and stare at the phone. Finally I pick up the receiver and punch in the code. I feel arms around my waist and know that it's Paul behind me, holding me up.

I listen to the message and grab a pencil, write down the number of the doctor and the lab, the time that they want me to come in for another blood draw. They say that they'll call by noon today to let me know for sure if I need to be retested. I hang up and turn in Paul's arms, feel the press of Jamie behind me.

Surrounded by my boys I can say it.

"Hep C."

Someone starts to shake and we all slide to the floor. No one says anything for a long time.

I don't feel sick.

Jamie finally gets up and then Paul. They drag me off the floor and we all go into our room, lay on the bed. At some point they both call in sick to work. I lay there thinking about the last time we all called in sick. Fred was pissed. He knew I wasn't sick.

Paul makes a huge stack of toast and we all eat on the bed, watch TV for a bit. When the phone rings I just about scream.

Jamie answers it 'cause he's closest. He hands me the receiver. "Think it's Fred."

"Hey Gent," I hear. "That Paul? Told you he'd stick close. Where the fuck did you go yesterday? Man was almost out of his mind."

"Bar."

"Yeah, I get that, I guess. They call yet?"

"No."

"Call me when they do, 'kay?" Then he's gone.

I crawl off the bed and go into the bathroom. Didn't think the toast was going to stay down anyway, what with all the booze in my system. Paul makes more and makes me eat.

The next time the phone rings I answer.

I listen and write shit down. Make an appointment for me and my boys to get tested. When I hang up they're staring at me, holding hands.

"Made appointments 'cause we need the reassurance. Too fucking scared not to get tested for everything again." I walk over to the them and touch their faces. So very much alike, these two. But they are so different. Paul's blinking too fast and Jamie's not moving at all.

"I'm okay. Really. They transposed some numbers.

Not sure if it was a bad test or what, but my blood is clean. They want to retest to make sure, but like I said, we're all getting tested again. I can work, if I want to. And—"

I don't get any further. Jamie falls back on the bed and starts shaking, curling up into a ball. Paul holds onto him and I fit myself around Paul. We don't say anything, just lay like that for a long time.

I call Fred later and tell him I'm taking the some time off, and that I want to talk to him about going appointment only. Afternoons. Three days a week.

"Can't live on that, Gent." He sounds skeptical.

"Don't intend to. Get another job somewhere. Just can't be working with blood right now."

"You're damn good at what you do. Think about it, Gent. You take care of yourself, keep working smart, you're not gonna catch anything. Don't let this throw you. Most guys ink for years and never get a positive for anything."

"Yeah. I know. Just give me some time to work this out, okay?"

Fred finally just gives in. "See you in a couple days. And we'll talk about it then."

Jamie and Paul spend a lot of time talking to me about why I don't want to ink. I try to make them understand that just because it turned out okay this time doesn't mean that there won't be a next time. That the thought of anything hurting them because of what I do makes me ill. That I would rather work at a job I hate than put them in any danger.

Paul doesn't like it. "You love what you do. You're good at it."

"Yeah. But – "

"Fuck this, Gent. I can die walking to work. Hell, I work at City Hall. You know how many disgruntled city employees there are? Stop being stupid and *think*."

I look at the floor. Jamie gets down in front of me, hands on my knees. "Gent."

I look into his eyes and all I can see is trust. And that just blows me away after last night.

"You take every precaution there is, right? You're careful. You're smart. There's guys out there who don't work with blood who take far more chances than you. I've seen you looking at your hands. You're obsessed with being safe."

I nod. Fight the urge to check my hands.

"So don't do this, okay? Go afternoons only if you want, but please, don't go out and get some crap job you hate just 'cause you're scared for us. Hell, I get cut up more than you just playing sports. See me after pick up basketball? Think, Gent. Do what you love."

"But I don't want you to get sick."

"Keep being as careful as you are. We won't. You won't."

I sit back in the chair and close my eyes. Think. Feel Jamie's hands on my legs, Paul's on my shoulders. I feel like I could sleep for days.

"Okay." I take a breath and think for a minute, or at least try to. "Afternoons only. See how it goes. Might have to get a night job somewhere, though. Maybe pull beer at the Edge, yeah?"

Hear a soft sigh and then Paul's kissing me. Hand at my neck turning my head and then Jamie's there and we've got one of those wonderful and strange three way kisses going on.

I'm just so tired.

We all go down and get tested. We all go down and get the results. And then we all go home, clean and healthy, and get really, really drunk.

Not sure what it is about being shit scared that make us all want to get shit drunk, but we do it. Don't even do anything else, just stare at the TV and drink beer, then rum. Eventually we order some Chinese food and try to get a little sober.

We talk about me going back to work again, but not for long. I'm still adamant about only working part-time and Taff gave me a job at the Razor's Edge so I'm making the same amount of money—a little more, actually, with tips.

Jamie still thinks I'm wasting my talent, and Paul still thinks I should do what I have to do for now, but hopes I'll go back fulltime soon. He misses me on the weekends, he says, but I suspect he agrees with Jamie.

"I just… I can't take knowing I can pass something on to you as easy as that," I try to explain for the seven hundredth time.

Jamie sighs and passes me the fried shrimp. "Nothing's changed, Gent. Nothing at all."

"I know," I say, gesturing with my chopsticks. "But that's the point. We were fucking reckless, boys, and I won't do that again. We gotta be more careful, not just go on like we were."

They exchange an uneasy look and Paul looks at me out of the corner of his eye and shrugs. There are times I hate that secret-twin-language thing.

"Um, Gent?" Jamie says slowly. "Wanna run that by us again?"

I set down my plate and lean forward. "We have to take better care of ourselves."

"Break it down a little more."

I sigh and Jamie shakes his head. "Just fucking humor

me, will you? What precisely are you suggesting?"

I look at him, then at Paul and back again. "Condoms. All the time, not just when we fuck."

Jamie's eyes do this weird thing, they go really wide and then really narrow. Paul just looks unhappy.

"No way," Jamie says. "In fact, I think we should ditch the rubbers altogether, now that we all know we're clean for sure and provable."

My jaw drops. "Are you insane?"

"No, but I'm beginning to think you are." He stands up, angry vibes just rolling off him. Paul looks less unhappy and more freaked than anything, his eyes darting from Jamie to me and back. Like he's watching the worst tennis game ever and knows it's going to end in carnage.

I stand up too. "Jamie, you can't be serious."

"I am. And I think you're taking this too far, Gent. I think you're letting your paranoia seep out and it's affecting us too, now. I won't let it, pretty." He's standing in front of me with his arms crossed and I get that horrible them-against-me feeling again.

Jesus, I thought we were past this.

I fall back on the couch and close my eyes. "This isn't a game, Jamie. You don't get to win by being faster or stronger—only smarter."

Jamie makes a noise that can only be called a grown of frustration. I open my eyes to see him pacing and Paul watching with wide eyes, biting his lip.

"Baby," I say. "Paul. I can't take the chance. Do you see that?"

Paul looks at me for a moment and then comes over and sits next to me, curling into my side. "Listen to me, Gent. Okay? Just for a minute. You too, Jamie. I want to tell you what I see, and I need to say it all. No jumping up and talking over me, or I swear to God I'll deck you both."

Jamie and I both grin before we can help it, though it doesn't stick around long. Just a whisper of light. We nod and I put my arm around Paul, kiss the top of his head. He tilts his head to look up at me and he smiles before pulling away. Without saying anything he goes to Jamie and kisses him, then gets Jamie to sit on the couch with me.

Suddenly, inexplicably, Paul's in charge, standing in front of us and looking like he's about to lay down the law. I think Jamie feels it too, he's already sitting straighter, like he's ready to jump up and walk away. I grab his wrist and give him a warning look. He rolls his eyes at me, but stays where he is and even leans back. And he holds my hand.

"Okay, this is how I see it," Paul says. He's crossing his arms across his chest, exactly like Jamie does, and I wonder vaguely if their dad did it too. "You two are opposite ends of a spectrum over this, and we have to find a compromise that works. Gent, you're freaked and worried and your instinct is to protect us, to do everything you can to keep us safe. I appreciate that, I do."

He smiles at me, looking encouraging and weirdly hopeful, so I open my mouth to say he's right, that I have to take care of them, and he tells me to shut up.

"Shut up," he says. Really. "Let me finish. You're being over-cautious and you're projecting your fears."

Oh, I am not!

"Jamie, you're being reckless. You're trying to prove you're fucking invincible or something."

Oh, he so is!

"I am not!" Jamie bursts out.

"You are," Paul insists. "And shut up. Now, look. Jamie, you're my hero, you know that. Don't you? You should know that by now." He comes a little closer and sits on the coffee table right in front of Jamie. "I know you're not going anywhere. I know you love me. And if sometime I have to sleep alone, I know I won't have nightmares." His voice gets real soft and he leans forward until their touching, staring into each other's faces. "You're always going to love me, I know, and I know you're not going to die or leave me, okay? You don't have to prove it anymore, don't have to do things just to prove you can live through it for me."

One of us sniffles, and I'm pretty sure it's one of them, but I wouldn't swear to it. It's wildly intense being a part of something that intimate, that heartfelt. Being allowed to be a part of it. Then Paul kisses Jamie and they both kind of rub at their eyes. I sniffle this time.

Jamie leans back and takes a deep breath. "Okay."

Paul looks at me and I hold up my hands. "Go easy on me, baby."

"Nope." He slides down the table until he's in front of me and then he kisses me too before looking at both me and Jamie. "Here's what we need to do. Gent, you're asking too much of us. We've never used condoms with each other, really. Just the odd time when the three of us have been together. You asking us to start using them all the time, despite clean tests, isn't going to fly so we need to find a compromise that will make us all somewhat happy."

He tilts his head at me and I open my mouth again, only to get the now-expected "Shut up." He might bottom a lot, but the boy isn't very subby.

Jamie's sitting back again, and I take his hand, which makes Paul smile absently. He's thinking, and therefore distracted-looking. It's kind of cute, actually, and sometimes it goes on for a while—not this time, though. He's only in his thinking place for a minute or so before he sits up straight.

"Gent, promise us you'll take every possible precaution

at work."

I blink, surprised. "Of course I promise."

Paul nods. "Thank you. That's your job. Jamie, I don't want you to use a rubber when you fuck me."

Jamie grins and Paul holds up his hand again and says, "But as long as Gent's uncomfortable about it, he can. As long as he wants. And if he wants to use rubbers when you two fuck, you let him. No arguments, and if you're in him you wear one until he says otherwise."

Jamie frowns and looks at me. Like I'm supposed to tell him I changed my mind or something. But he sighs and nods, and I squeeze his fingers as a thank you.

"Gent?" Paul asks carefully.

Uh oh. I sense a big flashing light of warning coming on.

"Yes?" I say, just as carefully.

"Did you *always* use condoms for blowjobs before us?"

Damn.

I sigh to match Jamie's. "No," I admit. "That usually fell into the acceptable risk category."

"Fine, it still is. So, I suggest—rather strongly—that we ditch the latex for that, all three of us, and you continue to use condoms at your discretion for fucking, with the understanding that we won't be. Reasonable. Yes?"

No.

Ah, damn it. Jamie and Paul are both looking at me, and I have no freaking idea why they don't see that they'd be much safer locked in a room and wrapped in plastic and never ever allowed out in public where something can hurt them.

Okay, I might be projecting.

"Fine," I say. Sometimes it's easier to give in than fight until they do. Besides, with my boys? The after-discussion sex is a lot of fun.

Chapter Nine

Being with twins, you learn a lot about three-way relationships. You learn how to suck and get fucked at the same time. You learn how to kiss in weird combinations. You learn that it can get strange when the two guys you're with have been together forever, literally.

And you learn that no matter how much they love each other, no matter how in love they are with each other -- and yes, there is a difference -- they are still twins. Which means that they are hot and sexy in the same way physically, and they are hot in their own ways, 'cause they're different people. It also means that they are siblings.

Are you listening to me? I mean, think about it. Sibs. Who fuck and fight. And when you fight with your lover, someone you trust not to leave, you can say some bad shit. When you fight with a sibling you say worse stuff.

They don't fight very often. They're too close, too much in love, to do it any more than once every few months. But when they fight it's bad. They scream and shout and curse and bring up shit that happened when they were twelve. One of them will finally have enough and storm out of the apartment, and then I'm left with one angry twin and a pain in my gut.

Usually, if I'm left with Jamie, we have a beer while he grumbles and moans and swears under his breath. Then he works it out in his head until it makes sense for him and we have a sympathy fuck until Paul comes home and they make up in some kinky twin way that I get to watch.

If I'm left with Paul he gets all quiet and depressed and I have to stay away from him until I can't take it anymore and I drag him off to bed, get him naked and just hold him until Jamie comes back. Then they make up and I watch. Then we all fuck.

But this time it's different. I'm left with Paul after Jamie takes off and he's not sad or quiet. He's really fucking angry this time, and he's aggressive and not like my Paul at all. I don't have a sweet clue what to do with him. So I ask.

"What do you need, baby?"

He stares at me from across the living room and then runs to me, throws himself across my lap, ass in the air. "Gent."

"Yeah?" I admit I'm a little confused. This is so not a Paul position and I'm not sure where to put my hands. I put one palm on his ass and wait, something uncurling in my belly that I don't quite get, but sort of do.

"Gent, I need."

"What do you need?" I keep my voice low and smooth, rub his ass, feel him start to get hard against my leg.

"Hit me."

I freeze, knowing he was going to say it, and knowing I can't do it.

"Paul. I can't hurt you."

He looks up at me then, his eyes wide and needy and full of something I just don't get. "Hit. Me."

I see he's serious, that he's not going to back down and that if I don't do this there is going to be a lot more than just twins making up later. And maybe I won't get the chance to do any making up.

"How do I know when to stop?"

"When I come on your lap."

Okay. Wasn't really expecting that, or the instant hard-on I get. I raise my hand and smack his ass, hard. He jumps and moans.

"Again."

So I hit him. Through his jeans and underwear, hard. Over and over, working into a rhythm that makes my hand sting and my arm sore. He's arching up into my hand when I bring it down and he's not making any noise at all. He starts to shake, and I stop.

"Look at me."

He shakes his head. "Hit me, Gent. Please."

"Not until you look at me, damn it." I hate this. I hate hurting him, I hate not understanding what the hell is going on.

He looks up and the need is still in his eyes, but he's turned on. The anger has faded and he's just Paul. Paul who really wants me to smack his ass and make him come.

"Take off your pants," I tell him, my throat dry.

He rolls off me and jerks his pants off, is back across my lap and I can see how red his ass is and it makes me wince. "You still sure about this?" I ask.

He nods and I start in on him again, and now it really does hurt my hand, 'cause skin makes it sting more, and oh, fuck he's getting red and it's so fucking hot the way he's twitching and moving, humping my leg and moving his ass back to catch the next smack. I'm so hard it hurts and I want him to suck me off so bad.

I hit him. Over and over and listen to him start to moan, making these noises deep in his chest and throat and I know he's close. I hit him lower, closer to his balls and he jerks on my lap and comes all over me, shooting again and again and again, gasping for air and clutching the pillows and fucking yelling.

I'm hard and I have to take care of my boy. I get him cleaned up and hold him for a bit, waiting for my hard-on to go away. I get some cream from the bathroom and rub it on his ass, being as gentle as I can, wincing when he moans. Oh shit, I must have hurt him, his skin is so red, and it looks raw and tender. God, how did I let him talk me into this?

I carry him into the bedroom, and no, it's not easy, seeing as how he's got about twenty pounds on me, but I do it. I get him all laid out on his stomach and he falls asleep, whispering a thank you.

I go back to the living room and clean up, sit there until Jamie comes home and sees me.

"What happened?" He's all concern and worry now, and I'm a little pissed off.

"He asked me to hit him."

Jamie, the fucker, grins and comes over, drapes himself across me. "Surprised it took him this long. Did you do it?"

I show him my hand and he kisses the palm and licks the fingers, making happy horny noises. "Did you get him off?" he asks around the finger he's sucking. My cock is hard again as I watch him use his mouth on me.

"Yeah. He came for ages."

He makes more happy sounds and shifts around, letting me feel how hard he is. "You get off?"

"No. I didn't like it." Yeah, I lie to my boys sometimes. Shut up.

He laughs. "Yeah, right." See? Makes no difference. They know me. "Well, then. What should I do for you?"

I arch up and grab his hand, put it where I need it most. "Suck me, Jamie."

He moves fast, to the floor between my legs and he's got my pants undone and my cock out before I can even get settled on the couch. I let my head fall back as he swallows me, working me fast and hard, like he always does. His hands are everywhere and his tongue is licking and tasting and I can't just sit, I have to move and he knows it. Paul takes his time when he goes down on us, but Jamie...Jamie likes it fast and hard and that's why I asked him.

I thrust my hips up and he lets me, just changes the angle so I can fuck his mouth better and he's sucking at me for all he's worth. His tongue is teasing and he's got one hand on my balls, rolling them and tugging gently and he sucks hard at the head of my cock. He gets his hand wet, sliding it over my shaft, following his mouth and then he's teasing at my asshole. I watch as I slide in and out of his mouth, his lips swollen and red, his eyes dilated and hungry and I know I'm close, can feel everything getting tight and hot. Oh fuck, so good, so right. I can see Paul's ass is in my head, red and raw from where I hit him, hear Jamie moaning around my cock, and I shoot down his throat, coming hard. He swallows it all then lets go, fast, pushing me back on the couch. A quick scramble in the end table, accompanied by curses about my fucked up sense of morals and he's forcing his gym pants down, a rubber on, and then he's in me. Christ it hurts, but it's so fucking good.

He's swearing in my ear about how fucking tight I am and how he wants to watch me spank Paul and when Paul's ass is better how he's gonna fuck him for me, and oh, shit, he's coming in me, so fucking fast and I haven't even gotten into his rhythm yet and I just want to go to bed and lie between my boys and forget the day has even happened.

I want a do over. I want to spank Paul 'cause we both want it, I want Jamie to suck me 'cause I need *him* to, not 'cause I need the release and I want to be with them both in our bed where no one is angry and we're all just warm and horny.

But then, that's what tomorrow is for.

Chapter Ten

It's Jamie's night to close the store so Paul talks me into going to a play with him before we meet up with Jamie and go to the Razor's Edge to shoot pool and have a few drinks. Now, plays aren't really my thing, which works out, 'cause this isn't really a play; it's more performance art. With naked people.

We're sitting there watching this... show, and I'm trying to figure out what the hell it's all about for the first bit. They aren't talking, just moving together in slow, slippery motions and I start to get sorta turned on. Which makes me think that I'm some sort of pervert. Then I remember who I live with, and figure that's okay.

Paul's just watching, not looking at me at all to see how I'm reacting. I watch him out of the corner of my eye for a bit and he's not doing anything other than watching the show, so I turn back and give it most of my attention, the rest being taken over by thoughts of what I'm going to do to him when I get him away from all the people around us.

Finally it's over and we can leave, except Paul wants

to stay for a bit and talk to someone he knows. So I sigh and roll my eyes and he looks at me funny.

"What's up?" he asks. And isn't that a good lead in?

I just tilt my head and look at him and he blushes. "Oh," he sort of gasps and then he grabs my hand and we leave.

I'm thinking that Paul has more than one kink, what with the spanking, which I'm sorta getting into, and this deal we have about alleys.

He drags me down the alley, between a closed grocery and a flower shop, and I can see this heading the same way it did the first time around. I roll my eyes and decide that this time he's the one who's gonna get slammed into a wall.

I spin him hard as we round the corner, and he's laughing. He knew I was gonna do that. Smart boy, my Paul. Or maybe he just knows me.

So I kiss him, and swallow his laughter, turn it into a moan as I get his pants undone. I nip at his nipple rings through his shirt and growl at him, start stroking his cock, already rock hard. Love that boy's willingness.

He's trying to talk, so I ease off and lean back, looking at his eyes. His pupils are dilated and there's only a hint of green at the outside. He's got one hand in his pocket and the other trying to undo my pants so I help out that hand for him and get my zipper down. He wraps his hand around me at the same time the other hand reappears.

The dear boy brought lube and rubbers.

"Do me," he says and kisses me hard before turning to face the wall, arms spread at shoulder height.

Not gonna turn that down. "Fuck yeah."

I get his pants down to his knees and mine down just far enough to suit up and squirt lube on my hand. I slick my erection and lean into his back, licking his neck. He shivers for me and I smile.

Chris Owen

"How do you want me, Paul?" I whisper. "Nice and gentle, like this?" I tease at his hole with a finger. "Or like this?" And I put my cock where my finger was and thrust deep into him.

"Oh Christ, yes!" Paul fucking hollers and then he's moving back on me, riding my cock hard.

I'm too worked up to play, so I hold his hips and just fuck him hard, loving how tight he is, how hot and right. He's moving with me, making noise and swearing and then he lets go of the wall with one hand and starts jerking off, fast and hard.

"Paul, yeah, do it. Touch yourself, fuck, so hot. God, want you to come, Paul." I know I'm babbling, but his ass is like a fucking vice around my cock and I'm so hard I almost hurt. My balls are tight and throbbing and I can feel everything in my spine get hot.

He shudders and calls my name as he shoots, spunk hitting the wall with a splatting sound and his ass fucking pulses around me and I slam into him, coming hard, practically biting his neck.

We're breathing heavy and I'm not sure my legs will move for a minute and then I slip out of his ass and he turns, real fast and kisses me hard.

"We gotta go see Jamie," he says, and my cock twitches. "We really gotta go get him."

I nod and he just looks so fucking hot and horny and well fucked I have to kiss him again. We finally manage to get cleaned up a bit, get our pants done up again and then we're off to go find our boy.

Paul and I manage to hail a cab after walking a block or so and head to the bookstore. Paul's vibrating next to me in the backseat and the cab driver looks worried, so I just smile and say, "Not drugs. He's just horny." The cab driver doesn't look reassured at all, but then Paul's kissing me so I don't care.

I fight Paul off most of the way to the store, but by the time we pay the cab driver and climb out onto the sidewalk we're both pretty wound up again. Still. Whatever.

Paul drags me into the store and we stand just inside the door, sort of giggling as Jamie looks at us. Except we're men. We don't giggle.

Jamie blinks at us. The store is just about to close so there's only about three people left. He shakes his head and mutters, "I don't want to know. Yet."

Paul giggles again. I smack him on the ass and we walk to the back of the store.

It's a nice place, with comfortable chairs and stuff here and there, tall stacks of books. It's part of a small independent chain, and has subjects outside the mainstream, which means there is only a small selection of mass market books. The rest is art, photography, some philosophy, a little local stuff. And the back wall is gay and lesbian literature and resources. There's only two other stores in the chain, one in New York and one in Dallas. Jamie runs the show here and the owners take care of the other two stores. Jamie likes to pretend that he doesn't read all that much, that Paul is the bookworm, but ask him anything about the books in here and you'll get an answer. He's a closeted bibliophile.

Anyway, Paul and I flop into one of the chairs and wait until the customers clear out before mauling each other. We figure if Jamie has to cash out and do some paperwork we'd just get bored waiting for him unless we entertain ourselves. Right?

So, I've got my tongue down his throat and Paul's making his happy noises with a hand up my shirt to get at my chain, and then Jamie's there, pulling my head back by my hair.

"What did you two do?" he asks, looking amused but undecided about whether he's going to kill us or not.

"Went to see a play," I say very mildly, and Paul snickers.

Jamie doesn't look like he's buying it. "Then what?"

Paul tugs at my chain and I gasp, roll my hips a little, 'cause it feels real nice, and I've been hard for ages, almost half an hour now.

"He fucked me up against a wall," Paul whispers, his eyes glittering.

Jamie sort of growls, deep in his chest, and kisses me hard, his tongue everywhere and I can feel one of them undoing my pants but I don't open my eyes to try to figure out which. Then there's a strong hand on me for a few strokes and I can feel Paul shifting around until he's gone from the chair. Jamie's still kissing me so I sprawl, letting the hand on my cock have as much access as its owner wants.

What its owner wants, apparently, is to suck me off, and therefore the hand belongs to Paul, what with Jamie kissing me and all.

I'm sitting in the chair, dick out, and pants halfway down my ass, Paul's on his knees in front of me. Jamie leans back and stops kissing me long enough to moan, "Oh God. Get his pants off, Paul."

I lift my ass and Paul hauls my jeans down, still teasing me with his tongue, licking and playing and Christ it feels so good. Then Jamie's behind Paul, reaching around and undoing his belt, lifting Paul's shirt up at the same time. I can see the light glint on Paul's nipple rings and decide that for our birthday I'm getting him a chain. A real nice one.

"Tease him, Paul," Jamie orders, getting Paul's pants undone and down. "Wait for me."

Paul grins, I can feel it. I moan.

Jamie gets Paul's dick out and strokes him. "God, you're so hard. Fucking hot, Paul." Then Jamie's undoing his own pants and fuck, I think he's harder than both of us. I groan as he leans down to kiss Paul's back and then he moves, comes around to kiss me.

"Where's the lube?" he asks into my mouth, and Paul sucks me hard in response.

"Paul -- Paul's jeans," I manage, but I'm not sure how. My hips are working, trying to get Paul to take me in, but he's obeying his twin's orders, waiting for Jamie.

Jamie digs the lube out and gets behind Paul, slicking his cock. "You ready, Paul?" he asks, but he doesn't wait for a reply, just eases in, nice and slow.

Paul shudders around me, and I see the muscles in his back ripple. I arch up into his heat and then, somehow, the three of us pick up a rhythm. I can feel it when Jamie moves into Paul, and I watch him, his eyes hot on mine while Paul sucks me. Oh fuck, it's amazing, so unbelievably good.

Paul's tongue is stroking at the underside of my cock, and every time Jamie pounds into him he takes me deep and sucks hard. I know when Jamie hit's Paul's sweet spot, I can see the vibration travel right up his spine.

Paul's moaning around me, and I'm saying shit like, "God, yeah, Paul. Like that, baby" and "Jamie, Christ yes, so hot, God, fuck him for me."

Jamie's just as bad, pouring words out for both of us, saying how hot Paul is, and how fucking sexy it is watching him suck me. He's right. There isn't anything better than my boys together. And watching them move, feeling them with me... fuck.

I lose it first, watching the twins go at it, being a part of it, part of them. I shoot hard and Paul swallows it, then Jamie's right there, a hand on Paul's cock, jerking him off as fast as he moves his hips, slamming into Paul's ass with sharp, wet sounds that send me reeling. Paul's pushing back, riding Jamie hard and I can feel his shudders building.

Jamie's eyes roll back and, oh fuck, he's coming hard, every muscle tight and he's groaning deep in his chest.

Paul's off me now and he arches his back, pushes back onto Jamie again and again and again, like he needs more and more and just can't get it. I slide off the chair and under him, take his cock in my mouth and that does it. He fills my mouth and tastes so sweet and bitter and just perfect, saying "God yeah, Gent. Oh, God, yes."

My boys are so hot just after they've fucked. So warm and sweaty and kissable. So I kiss them. They kiss me back and I can hear Paul murmuring his *I love you*s. I'm not sure who they are for this time, and I catch myself hoping.

Chapter Eleven

Jamie does a lot of things for me and Paul. He watches our movies and listens to us ramble about books all the time. So when he feels all restless and wants to play ball we let him talk us into a game of two on one.

Yeah, he kicks our asses. Basketball is so not my game. Nor Paul's apparently. We get back to the apartment all sweaty and hot, with assorted scrapes and bruises, and he makes us feel nice in the shower. It works out well.

We're in the bedroom later, nice and warm from the shower, naked and relaxed on the bed while we watch TV. I'm lying next to Paul, sort of curled around him, and he's sitting at the end of the bed with Jamie at his feet. He's brushing Jamie's hair.

Jamie's hair is at that stage where it's almost dry but still cool and silky and I'm almost mesmerized by the strokes as Paul brushes it. He uses long strokes, starts at the top of Jamie's head and pulls so slowly down to the ends. Jamie's hair is long enough that he leans back a little with each stroke and the swaying of his body is almost putting me to sleep. He's got a nice slow rhythm and I can hear the whispering sound the brush makes through Jamie's hair; soft and soothing.

The brush in Paul's hand pulls the hair away from Jamie, up Paul's body where it falls in a wave over his chest, sliding down his body. It's like a heavy curtain made of tiny threads, and Paul leans forward as it trails down his stomach, and reaches the brush out again to Jamie's head, starting over.

Jamie is sort of rocking with the motion, same was Paul, and I'm feeling kinda sleepy, but a little left out, so I get up and go to the dresser, get another hairbrush so I can do my own.

I turn around to walk back and stop cold.

Jamie's watching the TV, some monster movie. He's got his knees drawn up and he's letting Paul brush his hair, his body moving with the strokes, but he's not really paying attention, if you know what I mean. He's just sitting there, getting his hair brushed.

But Paul...

He's got his legs on either side of Jamie and he's pulling hair over himself, letting it cascade down, and he's fucking rock hard, his eyes glazed over and drugged.

"Shit, Jamie. You should see this." I stand there watching Paul and grin, then look at the brush in my hand. Jamie's trying to turn around to see his brother but Paul's stopped brushing, is using his hands to make Jamie look forward.

"What's he doing?" Jamie looks a little put out that he isn't allowed to see.

"He's getting off on your hair. Really. It's fucking hot."

"What? How?" Jamie doesn't look like he quite believes me.

Paul smiles at me and pulls Jamie's hair over himself again, shudders as the ends trail over his cock.

I use the brush in my hand on my own hair for a second and wink at Paul. "Like this," I say to Jamie and sit on the floor next to him, tipping my head down so I can brush my hair over him. I tease at his chest and belly, then drag the ends of my hair over his prick. He's getting hard, same as me, but I think it's more a reaction to Paul than anything else.

Jamie laughs and pulls me up to his mouth for a kiss. "That feels weird," he says. "Paul, you really getting hard back there?"

Paul drops a hand to his cock and strokes it once. "Oh yeah." His voice is tight and Jamie's eyes go wide.

I grin at Paul and kiss Jamie. "Gonna help him out. You're on your own, love. Think you can take care of yourself?"

Jamie raises a brow and sticks his tongue out at me. "Yeah, I think I know what to do. Idiot." He wraps his hand around himself and starts to jerk off, real slow, and I snicker at him before dropping one more kiss on his mouth and climbing back up on the bed.

Paul's watching me, still brushing Jamie's hair. I take the brush from his hand and settle beside him as best I can, so my hair is over my shoulder, dragging across his chest. I brush Jamie's hair and let my hair mingle with his, so Paul's getting sensation everywhere—his chest, his stomach and cock, down over his balls. It's kind of awkward, but after some maneuvering I find the easiest way to keep my balance and brush at the same time.

Paul's shifting around restlessly, and every time the ends of Jamie's hair tease down over his balls he shudders. He's making noises, low and soft, at the back of his throat, and I can hear Jamie's hand as he moves it over himself, still jerking off with slow long pulls.

"You better not fucking shoot all over my hair," Jamie says, and I can hear the smile in his voice.

I take a good look at Paul's cock and snicker. "You're gonna have to shower again anyway. He's leaking all over."

"Shit," he says, though he doesn't sound too put out.

I dip my head and lick at Paul, tasting him. Fucking heaven.

Paul moans and thrusts up, tries to get me to take him in. I pull away and drop the brush. "Tip your head back, Jamie. Let me play."

"You better be good to me later, pretty." Jamie's breath is coming faster, almost as fast as Paul's. These two get off on each other like no one else I've ever known.

"Will. Don't worry." I take a section of Jamie's hair and trail it over Paul, let it tease all over his belly before moving lower. Paul's got his hand in my hair, moving locks of it over his chest and I start to concentrate on wrapping his dick in loose tendrils, everything smooth and silky over and around him, soft hair teasing and playing as it slides.

Paul's breath is catching in his throat and his hips are starting to jerk, looking for friction. He can't find any and starts to moan, begging me to help him get off. I play a little longer, drag hair over his balls over and over until they start to draw up. He's gonna fucking come from this, and it's the weirdest thing I've ever seen. Hot, though.

"Gent. Please." He's whimpering now, and my own cock is throbbing.

Jamie moans. "Christ. So fucking needy. I wanna see him go."

I push Jamie on the shoulder, and he turns around fast, hair flying out around him. I swoop down, swallow Paul's cock and he thrusts up fast and hard a couple of times and then he's coming for me, shooting down my throat.

"Oh shit!" Jamie's kneeling beside the bed, watching and when he cries out I look at him, see him fucking into his fist, his eyes on me and Paul. Then he's coming too, fast and hard, pumping all over me and Paul.

I suck Paul until he starts to relax and Jamie crawls up onto the bed and kisses his brother, both of them twisting on the bed, tangling themselves up. I let Paul go and stand up, my legs a little weak and my cock hard, balls heavy.

I fall onto the bed, start rubbing off on Jamie. He rolls over and spreads his legs, pulling me on top of him. "C'mon Gent, fuck me."

"Rubber," I manage to say, pushing up against him anyway.

Jamie groans and Paul rolls away from us, reaching for the nightstand. He finds the stuff and then there are hot slippery fingers around me, rolling on the jacket and slicking my cock. I push into Jamie, just push into his tight hole and fuck, it's good.

Jamie grabs at his legs and pulls them up, opening for me, and I fuck him hard, need to come so bad. I rock into him again and again, hands on his hips, holding him down. I'm gasping for air and then I can just feel it come over me, just as hard and fast as I'm doing him. Lightning down my spine and then I'm shooting in him, riding it out, coming in stuttering jerks.

So fucking good.

I fall on top of him and he lets me get my breath back before rolling me over and off. He kisses me gently and gets up.

"Nice work, pretty. I'm going to go wash my fucking hair."

Paul's laughing as Jamie leaves and I wrap my arms around him, just holding on. He's warm and happy and I just want to crawl into bed and hold him. We kiss for a bit and he's still hungry, rubbing up against me, his cock getting hard again.

He reaches behind himself and picks up the hairbrush

and gives my hair a half hearted swipe with it before I start to laugh and grab the brush from him.

"Again? Not a chance, baby. Not gonna mess my hair up."

We're laughing together and rolling on the bed, fighting for the hairbrush. It's good and sweet and he's horny and I'm getting that way.

I get my arm around him and we stop playing, just lay there on the bed together, kissing. I move my hand down his back, stroke his spine with the back of the brush, all the way down over his ass and over the tops of his thighs. He groans into the kiss and thrusts harder against me, his cock practically drilling into me.

I do it again, less hand this time, more brush. It's a nice hair brush, not a cheap one from the drug store. It's Jamie's and I'm sort of thinking that Paul gave it to him. It's as wide as my hand, maybe more, and it's got a wooden back, smooth and warm to the touch.

I pull back a bit when he fucking bucks against me. "Paul?"

He just moans and thrusts against me, his eyes wide. God, he's kinky sometimes.

I sort of rub the back of the brush against his ass, pushing hard into his skin. "Want something?" I can fucking see it, smacking him with the brush. Would hurt though. A lot.

"Please." That's all he says, and then he's rolling over, moving back on the bed so his legs dangle off the end. Christ. I don't get why he needs this, why it gets him off, but fuck I want to do it. I want to do it for him, I want to do it 'cause he likes it, and I want to do it 'cause he was so hot last time. I'm getting into this, even though I don't understand it. Which makes me wonder about where my head is at these days. Getting kinks all over the place, and I can lay them all at his feet. Think lust and longing can twist your brain.

"Gent," he whispers. "Please. Need it."

I roll off the bed and walk behind him, kiss his spine and run my hand over his ass. As I stand up I put my free hand on his shoulder and squeeze it for a second, then I just haul off and smack him on the ass with the back of the brush.

"Yes!"

He loves it. He really does, and I almost see why, but not quite. I can't see his face, couldn't last time either, so I don't know what he really looks like, don't know what his eyes are doing. With my boy I can always tell what's what by his eyes. I feel sort of disconnected from this.

Until I get a rhythm.

My arm and hand are swinging and somewhere in the back of my head a voice is chanting 'one and two and smack, one and two and smack'. I can feel the strike when I connect all the way up my arm to my shoulder. All I can see is his ass, perfectly presented, getting red. All I can hear is the sound of my breathing and the low grunt Paul makes every time the brush hits him.

I don't know how long it goes on. I'm watching him carefully, still afraid that I'm going to hurt him, that I'll take him too far. I can hear his breathing getting labored, can see his legs start to tremble. He's lifting his ass every time to catch the brush where he wants it, the sounds he's making getting sharper and longer.

My hand is starting to hurt. My cock is rock hard, throbbing in time to the slaps. I can see his, straining in the air, thrusting forward with every smack, brushing the edge of the bed. His ass is red and raw-looking, practically glowing.

He starts to whimper. I change my aim slightly, hit him a little lower, making sure not to get too close to his balls, but low enough to hit skin that's tender.

He cries out and jerks, then he comes on the side of the bed, his entire body wracked with the shudder that passes through him. He drops one hand to his cock as soon as he starts to shoot, pumping hard, milking it. He's gasping and moaning, unable to say actual words.

I drop the brush and use that hand on my own cock, coming with a needy sound, unable to tear my gaze from my beautiful boy. He looks amazing, so full of life and pleasure, like a work of art. He's folded over the end of the bed, still trembling, tears on his face, still making those low moaning sounds.

"Jesus." Jamie's standing in the doorway, a towel around his waist, staring at Paul.

I look at him, meet his gaze when he finally stops staring at Paul.

"Jamie—" I don't know if he's going to be pissed or not. Paul and I aren't usually this intense when Jamie's home.

"Fuck, Gent. Have you ever seen him look so gorgeous? Christ."

I shake my head and go kneel behind Paul, gather him in arms. He's still out of it, trying to make his way back from wherever the hell he goes when we do this.

Jamie brings us some cream and together we tend to our boy's ass. Paul smiles at us and kisses me, then Jamie.

He doesn't say anything, just lets us take care of him, put him on the bed on his side. I lie down with him, careful to keep away from his ass, try to get as close to him as I can. I kiss his shoulder, and he smiles again, his eyes shining.

Jamie curls himself around me and I fall asleep with the heat of my boys surrounding me.

Chapter Twelve

The boys were right; this sucks.

I'm still working afternoons at the parlor and pulling beer at the Razor's Edge on Thursday, Friday and Saturday nights to make ends meet. The hours suck, the work sucks, the money sucks, and it's been going on for months. The only redeeming bit is that it's the Edge, and not somewhere else.

I like the place; it's just a dark beer room—pool tables at the back, a big square bar and a couple of TVs to watch the game on. It's not a dance club, so we don't get the college kids in pulling shit, and it's not a meat market, so we don't get every queer looking to get laid. That's not to say the college kids are totally absent—I usually wind up encouraging a couple of guys to take it back to the dorm instead of the back booths, and sometimes street kids come in to hustle, but it's an okay place.

Told Taff that if he's not careful the place will turn into a gay bar, instead of a gay friendly refuge. He said as long as the queens stay out, that's fine.

Because it's the Edge no one cares if my boys show up

and hang out while I work. They sit at the back and drink their beer, and when I can I go over and we talk about their days—that part's okay too. They shoot pool, and I get to watch them bend over a lot, which isn't anything to sneeze at. Half the time I drag them home, my dick hard enough to fuck them both into oblivion, the teases.

But right now they've sort of gone AWOL. It's past last call and the only people left in the place are Taff and about five of his buddies, all up in the front watching some soccer match in Europe. They're talking and smoking and just kicking back—I'm cleaning. Fucking love this part of the job. Not.

I've got to gather up the glasses and bottles and shit, then run the glasses through the dishwasher; the rest is just wiping the tables and making sure the pool tables are locked down—you wouldn't believe how much money the tables make. Taff likes to mop the floor after everyone is gone; he says it's his Zen thing. I just roll my eyes and am glad it's not me. As long as the tables are clean and the chairs are off the floor when I leave, he's happy.

So, I'm wiping tables, listening to the dishwasher and the music. We've got the volume down so the guys up front can hear the game, and I can hear them cheering and cursing. I head over to talk to the boys, tell them twenty minutes until we can go, and they're not there.

The horny little shits.

I've been watching them all night, sitting across from each other, flirting and teasing. I thought they were teasing me, but I guess it got too much for them and they've slipped into the bathroom for a little relief. Can't have that, can I? Them getting off and leaving me like this just isn't right. So I go down the little hall to the men's room and swing the door open.

The stalls are empty, and the place is just as barren as my Aunt Mary. Which, while not a nice thing to say, is true. So I cross to the ladies'. Now, the Edge doesn't get many women, but we have to have a ladies room anyway; it's just a single stall though—the door locks and it's just a flush, a sink and a mirror.

And it's locked.

So I bang on the door and flick the outside light switch off and on a couple of times. I'm leaning on the wall across from the door when they come out--Paul licking his swollen lips, and Jamie tucking his dick back into his pants.

Both of them are flushed and grinning and Paul pushes me into the wall and shoves his tongue in my mouth, letting me share the taste of Jamie's come.

"Evil," I say, rocking into him. Fuck, I'm hard. "Just evil."

Jamie leans on the wall beside me and licks my ear. "Got an idea, pretty boy. We're gonna play."

I sort of rub harder on Paul and smirk. "Yeah, we're gonna play. As soon as I finish up and we—"

"Nope, now." He's grinning at me and Paul looks positively demonic.

I push Paul away and stare. "No, we're not." No fucking way am I playing games right there. Not with Taff and his buddies up front.

"It'll be fun," Paul says, and he walks to one of the pool tables and picks up a cue.

I'm still standing in the hallway, trying to will my boner to go away. Hard to think when Paul's giving a stick of wood a hand job.

"It's like this," Jamie purrs at me. "Me and Paul are gonna shoot some stick."

I nod, watching Paul practically hump the pool table, his ass pointed at me, his hands working the stick like he'd like to do something really naughty with it.

"And you, pretty, are gonna fuck him for me." He says

it and then he's gone, leaving me standing there almost shooting in my pants.

"No, I'm not," I say. But I'm walking toward the table and checking out the line of sight from the front of the bar. Damn.

Paul's bent over the table, lining up a shot, and Jamie's on the other side picking out a cue. I stand right behind Paul and press my cock on his ass. "You want this?" I ask. Seriously. I know my baby has some kinks, but fuck, this is just stupid. And I'm just stupid and horny enough to do it.

"Oh yeah," he sighs, his voice real husky and low. He pushes back and adds a wiggle, settling my dick right in his crack. "Want to."

I look up. I can see the TV on the wall, can see the tops of six heads and I can hear them all talking. Can't make out words, but I can hear distinct voices, and all it would take is just one of them standing up to get a drink—or worse, walk back to take a leak—and we'd be caught.

I open my mouth to back out, tell the boys we'll play at home, when Paul looks over his shoulder at me and says, "Be so sexy, Gent. Want to ride you with them there, clueless."

And somehow I've got my hand in my pants, stroking my cock.

Jamie grins and comes around to us, rolling one of the pool balls across the table with the palm of his hand. He looks me in the eye and winks. "Got another surprise for you, pretty." He glances toward the front where we're being ignored by the men cheering some play on the TV. Jamie edges Paul back from the pool table and undoes his pants for him. "Baby's all ready for you."

I stare at him, not exactly sure what he means. Lack of blood in my brain makes me a little slow. Sue me.

Jamie's got his hand on Paul's dick now, stroking him

nice and slow. "Should have seen him," he says as Paul's pants fall around his ankles. "Stretching and slicking himself, riding his own fingers while he sucked me—"

I sort of phase out right about then, just rip my pants open and kind of tremble until I can get a rubber on. Then I just grab Paul's ass, part his cheeks fairly roughly and push right in. Jamie steps to the side and looks to the front of the room again when Paul moans and I gasp.

He's slick and fucking tight, can't spread his legs because of the pants around his feet, so I'm just pushing in with short strokes, eyes glued to the front where Taff and the others are. Paul's head drops down, he's not even pretending to line up a shot now, and he starts to curse.

I thrust hard, bury myself in him, and he grips the table. "No, no, no, fuck, not yet—" and then he shoots, coming as soon as I'm in him. His ass clamps down on me and he just fucking writhes on my prick.

I keep moving, keep fucking him, hands tight on his hips, sliding in and out and fucking nailing his sweet spot. He's trying to be quiet, but it's not easy—for me either.

Jamie's standing beside us and when I look over at him he's got his dick out, hard and red and sweet, his hand working himself fast. His eyes are wide, darting from Paul's ass to the front of the bar, and I look over at the men, feeling powerful and nasty and about ready to blow.

We need to do this fast, I know. Any time now one of them is gonna look up, one of them is gonna hear us—all I can hear is my panting, Paul's near-constant moaning, and Jamie's hand working his cock—and sure as fuck one of them is going to hear. But part of me wants it to last, to make it go on as long as I can.

I drop a hand to Paul's prick, still hard and getting harder again, wet with come, and start to pull him off. There's sweat dripping off the end of my nose, I'm so hot, and I just keep going, keep working him. I'm in my groove, the slide and grind and oh fuck yeah like that is taking over.

"Getting close," I grunt, and Jamie, I swear, whimpers.

He starts babbling about how we look, about how we're gonna get caught and for fuck's sake, pretty, just shoot.

I grin at him and say, "You first."

His eyes roll back and I look down at his crotch, watch him spurt his load all over Paul's leg, Paul's pants, and the floor. Then quick as anything he's doing up his pants and he's on his knees, licking his own come off Paul's leg. I just about go over.

I'm waiting though, waiting for Paul; I want him to come on me again, want to feel him dance on me. I plough into him, fucking him hard and fast, just Goddamn nailing him to the pool table.

"Oh fuck, Gent. Oh Christ," Paul moans, then he's spraying the table again.

Somehow, on a wing and a prayer I guess, I hold it. I freeze, feeling him around me, smelling them, waiting. I decide I must be a sick fuck after all, 'cause I want to get caught now, I want them to see us. Want someone to see me doing Paul over the pool table.

Then it happens. There's fire in my balls, my cock is throbbing and I can feel it. Going to come any second, no matter what I do. And a guy in front stands up and looks back at us.

I blow so hard there's funky lights behind my eyelids.

I don't think I even finish shooting before I pull out and Jamie's helping Paul pull up his pants.

Taff wanders back about eight seconds later. "You about done for the night?" he asks, looking at Paul. Paul looks totally fucked. I guess I do too.

"Yeah," I say, cool as anything. Except I'm leaning on the pool table, 'cause I can't fucking stand.

"Okay," Taff says, looking a little puzzled. "Don't bother locking the tables down, the boys and I are going to play for a bit, I think."

I sort of swipe the edge of the table with the rag I'd been using for the bar tables. "Okay," I say, hoping to fuck I got most of the come off. I drop the rag and push it around with my foot too, get the stuff on the floor. Christ.

"Your boyfriend all right?" Taff asks. "He looks like he's drunk. He didn't have that much."

I glance over at the boys as they pull on their coats. "He's okay, I think. Maybe the flu."

Taff nods. "Take him home and put him to bed. Tie him there if you have to."

Tie him... oh shit. "Yeah. I'll do that."

Chapter Thirteen

I want to say 'blame it on the book' or 'it was Paul's fault', but that would imply that I was reluctant, or that we did something that would make me feel like we shouldn't have. And that's not the way it was. So maybe it's better to say that it wouldn't have happened if Jamie didn't bring the book home and Paul's eyes didn't glaze over the way they did.

Paul and I are in the kitchen getting supper together when Jamie gets home from work. He's really late, more than an hour after we expected him, and he looks really tired. We fuss over him for a bit, make him eat supper and take a long shower, then we all curl up on the couch to watch TV. We're just getting into the Bruins game when Jamie remembers his present.

"Hey! Got a book from work you guys might like to look through," he says as he climbs out of the pile. Paul and I just kind of shrug and get closer together, share a kiss while Jamie gets this book for us to see.

He's right, it's something we like to look through. Big coffee table book of photographs. Nice naked boys with hard cocks and tan skin, and oh yes, look. They're fucking. Twos and threes, just what we like. So we flip through and critique their technique, make notes on stuff we haven't gotten around to yet. Then we see the picture that makes Paul groan in a needy way and I tear my gaze from the page to look at him.

He's staring at the book and I swear he's flushed and breathing fast already. I take another look at the book and look at Jamie, who's staring at Paul like he's never seen him before.

"Paul? You okay?" he asks. He's trying to sound like he's teasing, but even I can hear the tentative note in his voice.

Paul just nods and closes the book. "I'm gonna go take a shower," he says and walks away real fast.

Jamie and I stare at each other. That's not how shit works here; if we want something, need something, we just say so. So we follow him into the bathroom.

Paul's just getting the water going when we walk in and grab him, wrap him up the way only two people can. When he's between us I kiss him and then Jamie does.

"You like that, Paul?" I ask, and kiss his shoulder.

He sort of shudders and takes a breath. "Yeah, I think so. It looks… really intense."

"So why'd you walk?" Jamie says.

Paul just looks at him, his eyes real wide. "That's major shit, Jamie. I…"

"Didn't know how to ask," I finish for him, and they both look at me kind of surprised. I think it's the first time I finished a sentence for either of them, without tripping over the other twin.

So Jamie kisses him, and I kiss him and we all climb into the shower and get real clean. Then Jamie and I go to the bedroom and Paul gets even more clean. No one really says anything, but fuck, if Paul wants it then we'll do it. Same as if it had been Jamie.

Jamie and I lay on our bed, kind of snuggling until Paul comes in. Jamie, he's all relaxed and cool, just wants to make things good for Paul. So do I, of course, but Paul, he's hard and twitchy and his eyes are huge, so I gather him up in my arms and drag him down onto the bed, roll on top of him.

"You need to relax, baby," I say. "No way Jamie can do this for you if you don't relax a bit."

He nods at me and I kiss him, nice and slow, feel Jamie's hand on my back, stroking my spine softly. Paul's moving with me, and I kiss him harder, make him moan into my mouth, giving me soft needy noises.

"Jamie, I'm gonna get him off before you do this," I say as I move down Paul's chest, licking at his rings. "He's wound pretty tight."

Jamie just kisses a path up my back and moves to the side so he can take Paul's mouth with his, kissing him deeply.

I know how bad Paul wants to try this. He's never just taken off like that before when he gets an idea and I want him to know that he doesn't have to again. This is going to be intense and wild and I just want him to get everything from it he needs. Thing is, it isn't gonna work unless he calms down. So I don't waste any time getting him calm.

I move down his body and let Jamie take care of the gentling, let him use soft words and touches on his brother to get his head in the right place. My job, at the moment, is to relax his body. I lick at his balls and trace a finger down his cock. He's so hard it takes my breath away. I moan and shift, take him into my mouth and taste soap and him and just want to stay there for as long as I can.

His skin is hot and smooth and he tastes so good. He's heavy and thick in my mouth and I slide up and down his shaft, tease at the head of his cock with my tongue until he's thrusting into my mouth and I can taste the first drops of come leaking out. It's the taste that makes me wake up to the goal here, and I start to suck him, work him faster with my mouth and hand, feel his balls with the palm of my hand and then I can hear him breathe my name and he comes for me. I swallow him down and wait until he stops shuddering before I let him slip from my mouth and crawl up to kiss him.

"You ready?" I ask him.

He slides an arm around me and holds me for a moment then nods and gives me that fucking shy smile again. The one that makes me feel like I'd do anything for him. "Yeah. Thanks." He kisses me and then I roll away, looking for Jamie.

He's right there, like he always is, and I kiss him deep and hard. Then he's pressing me back into the bed and whispering, "We'll take care of our boy. You and me."

I nod and he's gone, down to the foot of the bed. He stands there for a moment, smiling at me and Paul. I wrap my arms around Paul and kiss him gently.

"Gonna make it so good for you, baby."

Jamie gets the lube from the nightstand and Paul shifts around so I can hold him, kiss him. Then he spreads his legs and Jamie is stroking the insides of his thighs, teasing and massaging him. I can feel him relax into my arms.

Jamie leans up and kisses us both, then he moves down, kisses Paul's belly as he slides two slick fingers into his brother. Paul moans softly, then sighs. "Feels nice, Jamie."

Jamie grins at him and twists his hand slightly and Paul's head drops back on my shoulder. "Oh yeah, there."

I run my hands over Paul's chest and belly, avoid touching his rings. We don't want him bucking and trying to get off yet. "So hot, baby. You're so sexy."

Paul turns his head and kisses me, our tongues playing and sliding and then he gasps again and I feel his hips thrust a bit. Three fingers. We stay like that for a bit, Jamie moving in Paul's ass and me kissing him, letting my hands be gentle on his skin. Then Paul whimpers and I look. Jamie's out of him, getting his hand real slick with lube.

"Gonna do this now, Paul," I whisper in his ear.

He turns his head to look at me, his eyes dark and round and full of something strong and needy. "Please. Please, Gent."

I hold him tight and nod at Jamie. Jamie takes a breath and shows me his hand, thumb folded in, then he starts to push into Paul.

Paul's watching. He's laying in my arms, watching as his twin slides his whole fucking hand into his ass. He's hard and twitchy again, so I whisper in his ear, kiss his face. I stroke his skin and try to get him to relax as much as I can, but he's just so fucking turned on I don't know if this is gonna work. Then Jamie slows down, stops, right at the widest part of his hand.

Paul's leaning on me now, eyes wide and unfocused, staring at the ceiling. "You okay?" I ask.

He nods and whispers, "Please. . ."

I glance at Jamie. He winks at me and puts his other hand on Paul's belly and I can see he's set to ease in deeper. Then Paul shudders in my arms and Jamie's hand just fucking slides in.

Jamie's eyes get huge. "Oh holy fuck, Paul. Holy fucking shit."

Paul is still. Perfectly, utterly still. Then he breathes and a sound escapes his chest and I want to fucking hear it again. Jamie looks totally floored, like he didn't really expect this to work. Then he gets a look in his eye and I kiss Paul gently.

"Paul? We're gonna keep going, okay? Gonna make you come."

Paul whimpers and I can see the muscles in Jamie's forearm work. He's making a fist, bringing his fingers in. Paul's shuddering and he looks at me with those wide eyes. "So full, Gent. Oh God, so full."

I nod and kiss him again, then watch Jamie. He's hard, real hard, and dripping. He's got the hand on Paul's belly working in a small, gentle circle, and he's got the other hand completely in his twin's ass and I think I have never seen any thing as beautiful as my boys.

Then Paul fucking starts to move. His hips shift a bit and he's Goddamn fucking himself on Jamie's hand. He's moaning and his eyes are wild and he's fucking moving.

Jamie gasps and stands real still, watching, not moving. Paul's doing it all. And then Jamie fucking comes. He's standing perfectly still, looking at Paul, and his cock just throbs, spunk shooting in ribbons onto Paul's leg. "Oh, fuck, Paul." Jamie's voice is full of wonder and his eyes are wide and staring. Then he starts to shake.

I ease Paul off my arm and scoot over to Jamie, hold onto him so he doesn't hurt Paul. He can hardly stand up.

"Fuck." I can't think of anything useful to say, so that's it. Paul, at least, has stopped moving.

"Oh God," Jamie whispers. "Gent, you gotta. Oh fuck. You gotta do this for him. For you." He's loose in my arms and I just look at him.

Paul makes a noise and we look at him, spread out on our bed, hard as a fucking rock with Jamie's hand still in him. He's staring at me. "Gent. Please. Want you. Need you, too."

I am beyond any sense. This can't be a good thing for Paul. He can't be fucking serious. But he is. I can see it in his eyes, in the way his body is fucking screaming for it, in the way he's looking at us both.

I get the lube and help Jamie ease out. Paul practically cries at the loss and Jamie kisses me hard and falls on the bed to kiss his brother. I slick my hand, using too much lube, and skip the two-three-four finger shit. I mean, why bother at this point?

I make my hand as small as I can and press against his hole, real loose from Jamie's hand. I slide in, real slow and easy, to my knuckles, and stop to look at them. Jamie is holding him and Paul's back to staring at the ceiling. I can feel him pushing down on my hand.

"Paul. Baby, you gotta stop. Let me do this for you, don't hurt yourself."

Paul shudders and I can hear Jamie whispering to him, soft words that seem to calm him enough that I can push, so fucking gently. And the same thing happens to me as Jamie. Just when I get the widest part of my hand at his entrance he just fucking relaxes everything and I slide in. It's unbelievable. And so fucking hot and tight.

I can feel his heartbeat. I can feel everything. I put my other hand on his stomach and I can feel him between my hands. I have my baby in my hands. My boy. I look at him and he's staring at Jamie and I can see so much passing there, so many years of them together, a lifetime. And it's beautiful and I am part of it because I hold my boy in my hands.

I curl my fingers together into a fist and flex, trusting Jamie to hold Paul, and trusting Paul to let me know what he needs. I'm so fucking careful I think I may break before I can finish this. I need to make it so good for him.

He starts making these noises I've never heard, something primal and desperate and full of need. I flex again and I can feel his hips move, so I wait for him, find his rhythm and go with it, press gently into him and feel him take it.

I'm fucking him with my fist and Christ it's the most intense thing I've ever done. It's beyond fucking, beyond making love, beyond anything. This is binding.

I touch his cock and he arches his back; I move my entire arm with him, keep the angle right. Then he's coming hard, shooting and shooting and fuck, I don't think he's ever going to stop. His entire body is spasming and grasping at me and he's still coming, his ass is holding me and I can feel his heartbeat.

I watch him. I watch Jamie. I can't do anything but stare.

Finally, the last shudder fades and he's limp and spent and I try to ease out of his body but he holds me there, keeps me in him. I look up at him and he's staring at me.

"Can I tell him, Jamie? Can I tell him now?"

Jamie nods and I don't have a clue what the fuck is going on. I just want to lie with my boys and let someone help me get off, feel their heat around me, taste them, be with them.

Jamie and Paul are looking at me, and I'm just staring back, still trying to ease my hand out of Paul without hurting him.

"We love you so much."

I moan and stare and oh fuck, I think I'm going to fall over and I don't want to hurt him, God don't let me hurt him and Jamie is just there and he's holding me up and he's helping me slide my hand out and he's saying it over and over and over.

I'm on the floor. The fucking floor. In Jamie's arms and I can hear myself saying it too.

"I love you."

Chapter Fourteen

It's Paul's turn to do the dishes so we all change our clothes after supper. Our boy likes to play, and apparently soapsuds are just irresistible. Jamie and I stopped hiding in the living room on his dish nights the first time he delivered the bubbles to us.

It takes a long time for couch cushions to dry.

So now we play cards at the table, the three of us dressed only in sweatpants, and wait for the water fight. 'Cause there is *always* a water fight.

Jamie's dealing the cards and I'm kind of grinning at the look on Paul's face. Jamie made lasagna for supper and I swear he used every dish we own. Except for the ones that have homemade oatmeal stuck on them from breakfast this morning. Yeah, it was a good day for food here. Kinda sucks for dish duty though. Paul's not too happy.

Matter of fact, I think Paul's pretty pissed. He's done a sink load of pots and pans, cleaned the sink and refilled it, done the plates and glasses, drained and cleaned it again. Now he's doing the cutlery, and Jamie and I are still dry. Completely soap free. We even made it all the way through three hands of Rummy.

Paul's not saying much, just doing the dishes. I glance at Jamie and he kind of shrugs, so I get up and go over to Paul, stand behind him and put an arm around his waist, just hold onto him.

I kiss his neck and ask him what's wrong.

"Nothin'. Almost done here." He leans back into me, but his voice is…well, my boy sounds tired and put out and like he needs cheering up.

I reach out and grab the hand cream off the kitchen counter. They smiled and just shook their heads when I started leaving hand cream at all the sinks in the house, but I hate having dry skin on my hands. Ever have to wear latex gloves most of the day? Not fun if you start out with dishpan hands.

I pour lotion into the palm of my hand and start spreading it over Paul's back, just rub his shoulder blades a bit. He's pushing back into my hands, his head dropped down, so I guess it feels okay. I do that for a couple of minutes, not long, then I just slide my slippery right hand into his sweatpants and cup his balls. Paul doesn't say anything, just leans back into me and spreads his legs a little.

"Like that?" I whisper into his ear, and he nods his head. I squeeze his balls gently, feel him start to get hard. I keep playing with his balls, lick and kiss his back and neck until he's hard for me. When I move my hand to stroke him he moans a little.

I'm rubbing up against him, my cock hard on him, lined up with crack in his ass. My other hand is slick with the cream too, and I slide it easily around to his chest, play with the chain connecting his nipple rings, tugging carefully.

His cock is heavy and full in my hand, so hard and hot.

My boys have gorgeous cocks, long and thick. Paul's hips are moving, pushing his prick into my hand, brushing his ass against me.

I groan and grind my cock into him, give his chain one last tug before I slide my hand down and back, pushing his sweatpants down.

"Gonna be in you, Paul."

The answering moan comes from beside me. Jamie's leaning against the stove, legs spread, hand on his cock over his pants. His eyes are hot on me and my breath catches in my chest. Love it when he watches us.

Jamie looks me in the eye and swears, then he's on his knees, pulling Paul's gym pants all the way down and off, then mine. I step out of the sweats and Jamie's got his mouth on me, just the briefest flash of heat and suction, then he's standing again, thumbs hooked in his waistband. He holds my eyes with his as he strips.

Paul's watching him and his hips are working faster, his cock leaking over my fist. "Kiss me," he says to Jamie, and they're locked together, mouths wide and wet and I can see their tongues lapping and twisting.

Jamie pulls away and pretty much lunges for the drawer on the end where we keep our kitchen stash of condoms and on the way back to me he grabs the lotion. He moves behind me and gets me ready, slick as anything; I swear we've got this whole "condom on, lube up" thing down to about four seconds. He doesn't waste his time, probably scared I'll blow before I do Paul. Just as fast he shifts and has two slick fingers in Paul's ass. We all groan, and I feel so fucking alive.

"C'mon, Gent," Jamie says. He's trying to suck my ear off, I think. "Make him feel so good."

He pulls his fingers out of Paul's ass and strokes me a bit, then he guides the head of my cock right to Paul's asshole and I slide right in.

"Oh yeah, so good, Paul."

He's tight and hot and soft and hard and fuck, he's so sweet. Nothing on earth as good as being with my boy. Nothing better than feeling him around me.

I start to fuck him nice and slow, just pushing in and feeling him shudder around me before pulling almost all the way out. His cock is so hard, his balls heavy and full. His skin is salty with sweat. Love this. Fucking amazing.

"So good, Gent. Yeah, so good." He's holding onto the edge of the counter, hips rolling back to ride me. Fuck, he's so tight, so beautiful. He turns his head and I kiss him, one hand on his hip, pulling him onto me, the other on his cock, stroking him as I fuck him.

Jamie's hand glides down my back and he presses into our kiss. I get lost in the taste of them, the way Paul feels around me, the heat of their bodies holding me close. Jamie nudges my feet further apart and the hand on my back moves lower, strokes my balls.

"Jamie." I can't say anything else, I'm too wired, need something and don't know what to ask for. He slides his fingers into my ass and I freeze, try so fucking hard not to come. Grip Paul's hip tight, don't let him thrust back onto me. Then the feeling fades and Jamie fingers me while I move with Paul.

Jamie moves my legs even further apart, kisses my neck. Then the fingers are gone and he's pushing his cock into me.

"Oh fuck! No, too soon, oh shit! Don't want to come yet!" I'm practically crying.

He holds my hips and says, "Don't move. Hold on, Paul. Try real hard for me." Paul freezes, whimpering.

Oh Christ. Jamie moves into me so fucking slowly, filling me, stretching me. When he's deep in my ass we all just sort of breathe for a moment, then he puts a hand on Paul's hip and pulls him back onto my cock.

"Oh God." I feel like I'm going to fly apart. Jamie pulls out a bit and stops. We're all holding our breath and then I move, thrust into Paul, back onto Jamie, fucking myself on my boys.

It's too much. Tight heat around my cock, Paul's ass clamped on me like a fucking vise, hearing him whimper and moan. He's got a hand tangled with mine on his cock, trying to slow me down. Jamie in my ass, balls deep, filling me so perfectly, the head of his cock gliding over my prostate.

"Can't…" I manage to say. "Can't do it. Gonna go off too soon."

Jamie bites down on my shoulder. "Stand still, pretty. Let me." He moves back and pulls Paul onto me at the same time, then reverses it so when he slides in, fills me and hits my sweet spot, Paul's ass is pulling on my cock. There is such a careful rhythm to it, it's like dancing, except I'm standing still, just getting fucked and loved and held and treated.

Still too much and I speed up my hand on Paul's dick. "Yeah, so good. Fuck me, Jamie." Jamie speeds up too, pulling and pushing and there is lightning traveling up and down my spine and my balls are tight and full and fucking throbbing.

"Fuck, yes!" I scream, then I'm coming hard, pumping into Paul's ass and pulling at his cock. "Fuck, yes. Oh God. Come for me, baby, please, Paul!"

With a grunt and a long deep moan he does, spilling over our hands and then he's shaking and twitching and pushing back on my cock, his arms braced to take my weight.

I lean on his back and fucking near cry, I feel so good. Jamie's slamming into my ass, chasing his own orgasm, and I want him to fill me so bad. He's groaning and holding us, his hand meeting ours and getting slick with

Paul's come. He smears it on Paul's chest, then pulls his hand away and licks it while he's fucking me and that sends him off.

He comes for ages, throbbing in me, pulsing and shooting.

We're all gasping for air and I shift a little, ease out of Paul. Jamie's still buried in my ass, and I want him there. Paul manages to turn in my arms and we're kissing, easy and wet and sloppy, all three of us.

"Better, Paul?" Jamie says.

Paul just smiles. "Yeah."

"Love you."

"Love you."

"Love you."

Chapter Fifteen

W hat's your schedule like next week?" Jamie asks me. We're sitting at the table in the kitchen having supper on a Sunday night, just finishing up.

"Same as always," I say, wondering why he's asking. Paul's looking pretty curious too.

"No, I mean appointments. You got any late afternoon times open?" Jamie's looking kind of eager, and it's pretty obvious he's being waiting a while before saying anything. He's sorta vibrating a bit. It's actually kind of cute.

Paul looks at him. I look at him. Then they both look at me.

"Uh, yeah, I think so. Can always go in on my own time though, if I don't. You wanting something done?"

Jamie nods and Paul stares at him. "Know what I want for our birthday."

"Our birthday isn't until next month," Paul says, biting at his lip. Uh oh. My boy isn't sure about his brother getting marked up.

"Want it healed by then," Jamie says, looking at his

plate.

I nod. "Makes sense. You got something picked out?"

"Yeah, but I need your help. Can't draw for shit."

I smile and Paul sort of snickers. It's true, Jamie can't draw a straight line, let alone a circle. "Sure, love. I'll see what I can do."

We finish up supper and Jamie does the dishes, fast and easy. No water fights on his dish nights. We all go into the living room and Paul flicks through TV channels, not settling on one for more than three seconds.

Jamie goes over to him and takes the remote away from him, kneels down in front of him. "What's up?" he says softly.

"Just never knew that you were even thinking about it. It's weird not knowing something about you." Paul's looking at the floor.

"Hey, look at me, baby." Paul looks up and I try to be real quiet, wish I wasn't here. This is one of those twin things, I think, and I always feel like I'm intruding when they talk to each other like this.

Jamie slips a hand inside Paul's T-shirt and tugs at one of his nipple rings. Hell, even I feel that. Start to get hard, and feel guilty. This is their moment, I tell myself.

"You did this for me, right? Surprise for me?"

"Yeah." Paul's trying to sound serious, but I can see his hips start to rock as Jamie plays. Watch him get hard.

"Same deal, baby. Well, almost, seeing as how now you know."

Paul gasps a little and arches his back, moves into Jamie's touch as fingers move over his chest, playing with his nipples. "What are you getting?"

Jamie grins at him and winks at me. "Now, now. Tell you that after we decide where to put it, yeah?" He lets go of Paul and stands up, grinning at us. Then he runs, heading for the bedroom.

Paul and I are right behind him, and by the time we tackle him and get him on the bed, we're all hard and horny and ready to play for a bit.

Jamie's laughing as we get him spread out on the bed. He's a little ticklish. I quirk an eyebrow at Paul. "So, what do you think? Get the canvas ready for inspection?"

Paul nods happily and works at Jamie's pants while I pull the sweatshirt off over his head. We get him naked fast and stand back to admire the view. I wrap my arms around Paul, standing behind him. "Pretty, isn't he?"

Paul wiggles his ass and grins when I gasp. Fuck, I'm so hard. "Yeah, he's pretty. So's the artist." Then he turns and kisses me, fingers at my waistband. He gets my jeans open and strokes my cock, moaning into my mouth.

I thrust into his hand, wanting him so bad. Want his mouth on me, want to fuck him, want it all and now. But he lets go and pulls off his own shirt, and that's okay too. I lick at his nipples, arms around him, pulling him so close to me he has to arch his back and bend over so I can tug at his rings with my teeth.

"God, Gent. Feels so good." He grinds against me and I have to let go, have to get him naked. I strip off his jeans and see Jamie on the bed, hand wrapped around his cock as he watches us.

"Canvas is getting impatient," I say to Paul, and Paul turns to look, his eyes hot on his twin. I get undressed and move behind Paul again, arm around his waist. "Where should we start, baby?"

Paul licks his lips and looks Jamie up and down. "Obvious places first, I think." He moves to the bed and climbs on, kneeling on Jamie's right. I follow, stretch out on his left.

We move our hands over him, stroking one place first, then another. "Biceps are pretty easy," I say, licking said muscle.

"Not personal enough," Paul answers. "Maybe here." He licks Jamie's chest, just above his nipple.

"Heart is on this side." I bend my head, lick the other nipple and move over a bit, suck up a mark over Jamie's heart. Jamie moans and runs a hand over my back.

"Soft skin here." Paul's kissing his way down Jamie's side, hands stroking at his stomach.

I shift all the way down the bed, massage Jamie's leg hard. "Calf muscles are good too. Maybe higher, here on his thigh." Jamie's hips are moving, trying to move with us, but we don't have a rhythm, we're just exploring.

Paul moves between his legs and licks at the inside of his thigh. "Here?" he asks, then bites lightly. Jamie groans. Paul moves up a couple of inches. "Or here?" Bites again, and Jamie's got the sheets twisted in his hands. Paul moves again, and I spread Jamie's legs.

"Not here, though." He licks at Jamie's ass, moves up to tease the soft skin of his perineum and up to his balls. "No, not here."

Jamie gasps and tosses his head as Paul starts to suck on his balls. "No, not there. That's Gent's place. Not my neck either."

I look at him, not sure what he means. He's never said he didn't like my tattoos, and I want to believe that he's turning down the spot 'cause I already did it, 'cause it's special to me. He meets my eyes and smiles at me, and I decide to go with that. Plus, there's the fact that I won't ink him there. Too fucking painful, and I won't do it to him, not if I can do it somewhere else.

Paul's still sucking at his balls and I can see Jamie's eyes start to roll back in his head. I run a hand up Paul's back and get closer, kiss Paul on the shoulder before I lick Jamie's cock. When I take him in my mouth he bucks up and I moan at the taste of him, lap at the come leaking from the head and just suck him down.

"Oh fuck. Please, pretty. Christ!"

He's moving now, and Paul's moaning, one hand trailing paths under Jamie's ass, the other reaching for my cock. Paul's hand wraps around me and I groan, then Jamie fucking screams as Paul pushes a finger in his ass. He comes hard, and I swallow around him, licking and pulling at his cock, wanting it all.

Paul's still stroking me off and as soon as I let Jamie go from my mouth he pushes me down, moves between my legs. I get about two seconds warning and then Paul's mouth is around me and I'm bucking up into his heat and oh fuck it's so good, so right. Jamie kisses me and I come hard, shooting deep into Paul's mouth, Jamie's tongue fucking my mouth.

Paul lets me slide from his mouth and then he's kissing us, one of those mind bending three way kisses that drive me insane. I can taste myself, taste Jamie. Then Paul's pulling us all apart, getting Jamie to roll over. He kisses him on the shoulder blade. "Here, Gent?"

I grin. Back to examining the canvas. I shake my head. "No, babe. Not there." Because now I know where I want to mark him, if he's willing.

Paul moves down, kisses a wet path down Jamie's spine. I reach for the lube and slick both hands. Paul's hard, really fucking hard, and Jamie is in just the right position. Rare treat to watch this.

I get behind Paul and slick his cock with one hand and tease at Jamie with the other. They both moan and Paul's fucking twitchy. Not much time, so I slide a couple of fingers into Jamie's ass as Paul licks at his spine. Jamie's thrusting back onto my hand, and I stretch him, reach for that one spot that'll get him hard again, and find it.

He bucks up and Paul sucks at the base of his spine, raising a mark just below his waist. "There, Gent."

"Yeah, baby. There."

Jamie groans again and moves on my hand, so I kiss Paul hard and move back, let him get ready. He settles close to Jamie's ass and I ease my fingers out, and just as easy Paul's in him. I stretch out next to Jamie and kiss him hard, feel him shudder as Paul moves inside him.

"Oh fuck," he whispers. "So fucking good, Gent. He's so good."

I smile at him. "Yeah, love. He is." I kiss him again and move back, get on my knees and kiss Paul, one hand on his ass, the other around Jamie's cock, and I move with them.

Paul comes first, thrusting hard into Jamie and crying out into my mouth. "God, Jamie. Now!"

And Jamie comes for him, right then, just shoots over my hand and I can feel them both shaking, Jamie's cock pulsing in my hand and Paul's ass clenching under my hand. So fucking hot and right and perfect.

They collapse onto the bed and breathe hard for a bit until they calm down. Then Paul rolls off him and Jamie makes a face. "Fucking wet spot."

I start laughing and can't stop, even when he pushes me off the bed. He strips the sheets off and throws a pillow at me.

When I get myself together again we all curl up on the bed around the pillows. "So, there, Jamie?" I ask, one hand on the mark that Paul made.

Jamie nods his head slowly. "Yeah. That's good."

"So what do you want?" Paul asks, his eyes bright and curious.

Jamie looks at him and pulls him close. "A 'P'. Want Gent to mark me with a 'P'. And I want him to sign it. Want him to put something on me that says I'm yours. And his."

Paul moans and kisses him hard. Jamie goes with it,

kissing him hard and deep, finally breaking the kiss to say, "Fuck yes, baby. Yours."

Paul kisses him again. "Mine. Gent's."

Jamie looks at me. "Yours."

I can't kiss him hard enough. "Mine. Yours." I reach for Paul and we're saying it again and I can't get enough of them, we're fucking sliding and rolling and rubbing all over the bed and we're touching whatever we can and it just goes on and on.

Not sure who comes first, but it doesn't matter. We all go over together, no names cried out, just the endless repetition of "yours" and "mine".

I've been lugging photocopies of alphabet scripts back and forth from the tattoo parlor for days, and Jamie brought home some books from the store, but we can't seem to find the "P" that he wants.

"It's close to this kind of thing," he says, pointing an old English script, "but it's not calligraphy, it looks more... carved. Sort of like it's etched, you know?"

I grab a pencil and start sketching. Takes me about a hundred sheets of paper, or at least damn close to it, but I finally get something that he's happy with. Mostly. I'm about to growl in frustration, but I remind myself what this is. It's a statement like nothing else I've ever inked. It's important, and it's special, and it damn well better be exactly what he wants.

He takes the last sheet from me and puts it on the coffee table. "It's good, pretty."

"But not perfect."

"Near it." He looks at me and smiles, then shrugs. "Wish I could draw."

"Me too, love. Me too."

We're still sitting there on the couch when Paul comes home. He wanders over and glances at the sketch before he leans down to kiss me. He tastes like grape pop. I suck on his tongue until he moans and pulls away to kiss Jamie. He settles in my lap and pulls Jamie over until we're all tangled up. Which is always good.

Paul kisses me for a bit more and starts to wiggle his ass. Fuck, he's hot. So sweet. I run my hand over his chest, tease at his nipple rings. He twitches and sighs into our kiss and I drop my hand lower, tug his shirt out of his jeans, pushing it out of the way. As sweet as his mouth is I want to hear him when I lick at his rings and tug at them with my teeth. He's moving faster on me and I let my hand drift lower, feel Jamie's fingers around Paul's cock. Just about come in my jeans.

I pull away from Paul's mouth and turn my head to take Jamie's kiss. His kiss isn't so sweet tasting, but it's all him—hot and fierce and intense. I rock my hips and rub my cock on Paul's ass. Jamie licks at my lips before breaking the kiss and moving away. He shifts on the couch and bends his head low to take Paul's prick in his mouth.

"Yeah, Jamie. Fuck, so hot."

Paul's got his eyes closed, his head tipped back. He looks like he's in fucking heaven, just blissed out. Makes me ache. I get him to lift his arms and get his shirt off, take the closest nipple into my mouth and tease it with my tongue, my lips, my teeth.

Paul's fucking close to losing it, his hips pistoning on top of me as he thrusts into Jamie's mouth, making these unbelievable noises. I can hear Jamie's mouth on him, sucking wet sounds that are going to make me come from just imagining how it feels. I can hear Jamie humming, or moaning—hell, I don't know what he's doing, but mixed in with Paul's soundtrack of "Oh shit", "God, yes", and

"Please, harder", it's about to send me over.

I'm rocking with Paul now, my cock so hard it hurts when he thrusts down, and Christ, but if he doesn't shoot soon I'm gonna come in my pants.

Jamie's got one hand tangled with Paul's and the other is undoing his own pants. The sound of the zipper going down is the last thing I hear before I cry out and fucking buck against Paul, coming hard. I just ride it out, head on the back of the couch, letting Paul fucking ride my lap like it was my cock up his ass. He's got his hand on the back of Jamie's head and I watch through half closed eyes as he fucks Jamie's mouth, cursing a blue streak.

Jamie doesn't quite get his cock free from his pants before he's shooting. He really fucking gets off on Paul taking charge. I think Paul's the only one who can actually top him without it turning into a big internal struggle for him. Which is cool, I get to watch.

Paul's still hard, still trying to get off. Jamie finally raises a hand to me and I lick his fingers while Paul watches, his eyes hot on my mouth. Then Jamie brings his hand down and teases it between Paul's thighs, still sucking hard on him, and slides two fingers in.

Sends Paul over the fucking moon. I hold my boy while he comes, not even making a sound. It's like he used up all the sounds and words he had, now he's just going on sensation.

Goddamn, I love him.

We are a big mess when we finally come down, clothes half off, come on the clothes we're still wearing…real pretty.

Paul reaches out and snags the sketch. He holds it out to Jamie and says, "Almost like the one on Dad's ring, isn't it? Not quite, though."

Jamie looks like he's been hit with a truck. He gets pale then flushes before finally just closing his eyes for a long time. Paul looks at me, eyes wide. I don't have a sweet clue what to say, if Jamie's upset 'cause of their dad, or what. I just hold onto my baby boy and wait.

Jamie finally opens his eyes and looks at me. "Sorry. I'm an ass. I knew I'd seen it before, I just didn't remember where, and you've spent all this time and—"

I let go of Paul and pull Jamie to me, shut him up with a kiss. "Don't be sorry. Not a big deal, love. Now you know where you saw the 'P' you want, yeah? So tell me what it looked like and I'll sketch it. Paul can help, too."

Paul's already standing up, going to the china cabinet. Yeah, we have china. And real silverware. Anyway, Paul gets a folder out of one of the drawers.

"What's that, baby?" I ask.

"List of the stuff in the safety deposit box. When Mom and Dad died Gran made sure we kept out the stuff we could use and put the rest in the safety deposit box. Things like Mom's wedding ring, the rest of her jewelry—you know, things seventeen-year-old guys don't wear." He looks up at me and grins before going back to the list.

Jamie leans into me and holds out his right hand. "I wear Dad's wedding ring. Paul's got his signet ring. The rest of his stuff is either here or in the box."

I nod. All I ever got from my dad was a box of rubbers and a really late curfew. Mind you, my dad's still alive. Think the boys would trade everything to have their parents back.

Paul closes the folder and puts it back in the drawer. "Not in the box, so it should be in here somewhere." He starts poking through cupboards in the cabinet. "Hey, did you know we have two teapots?" he asks over his shoulder. Jamie just shakes his head and kisses me.

Finally he comes back over with a small wooden box and sets it on the table in front of Jamie, who just reaches out and opens it. It's a small box really, only has a half dozen things in it. A picture of the twins when they were babies, a pocket watch engraved with the name "Peter", some cuff links and a silver ring.

Jamie picks up the ring and looks at it before handing it to me. "There it is. Do that for me, pretty."

I take the ring from him and sit back. It's heavy, really nice work. It's been hand-tooled, everything carved into it. The band is like a vine with tiny ivy leaves etched into it, and there is a flat circle on the top. It looks like there was a single ivy leave carved there at one point, but it's been worn nearly smooth. On the right side there's a raised "J" in stark relief to the vine, and on the left is the "P". It's gorgeous.

I don't even look at Jamie or Paul, just grab the paper and start sketching. I'll get this perfect for them or go blind trying.

I can't do Jamie's tattoo after hours 'cause of insurance shit, so the boys meet me at work after supper one night and wait until my shift is done. Fred says sure, use the chair on your own time, and says hi to Paul. I pull the curtain across the room, so the three of us are alone and get Jamie settled, lying on his stomach, jeans down around his ass. I bend down and lick his spine, making him shiver. I can taste soap and clean skin and need. I shiver too.

Paul's smiling at us as he hands over the sheet for me to photocopy. We've got the "P" the size we want, and I signed my name at the bottom, nice and neat. If my name is going to be on my boy I want it readable. I'm halfway to the photocopier when I see the change. Jamie wrote "love," above my name. All three of us into one tattoo. My throat feels tight and scratchy, but I don't say anything.

I get the image transferred to Jamie's back and move in front of him. "You ready, love?" I whisper. Fred is on the other side of the curtain.

"Ready for ages now. Love you," he whispers back. Then he kisses me and I step back, kiss Paul. I get my gloves on while the twins kiss each other and I think I need to stop thinking about this and just do it. Can't do the work if my hands are shaking.

The outlining is black, every curve perfect, every line smooth and easy. I ink over my name and then stop, catch Paul's eyes just before I do the word "love".

"Love you," he mouths.

I smile at him and get back to work.

Jamie's dealing well. It's never painless to get a tattoo, and I'm working real close to bone, his skin tight over his spine. Got to hurt, but he's not saying anything about it, just talking to Paul.

I get the outlining done and kiss them both again. I can hear Fred finishing up with his client right next to us and I hope he's done for a bit. We're open for another few hours, but it's a slow time of the day. All the after work crowd has been in and gone and it's too early for the ones who come in before going to the clubs.

"Gonna do the color now, Jamie," I say. He nods and I load the needles. This is the actual work part; the shading is what will make it look carved, give it life. And the color is just fucking gorgeous. Green, like ivy leaves, as close to the color of their eyes as I can get.

Takes me almost an hour. It's not real big but there're lots of angles, lots of planes to get just right. I'm completely into it, lost to everything but the ink and Jamie's skin. I know that Paul and Jamie are talking, but I'm not paying attention, just adding their voices to the background.

When I'm done I wipe him down carefully, make sure

I get all the blood off, and swab him with antiseptic. Everything is real careful and slow, I'm still working myself out of the headspace I get into when inking. I glance up and see Paul watching, biting his lower lip.

"Come see."

He steps around and takes a look, his eyes wide. "God, Gent. It's beautiful." Then his mouth is on mine and we're kissing nice and deep. I let him go when Jamie clears his throat.

Paul laughs and I grab the Polaroid camera and take a picture, hand the card to Jamie to watch as it develops. I'm about to kiss him too when I see Fred, standing against the wall. I've got no fucking clue how long he's been there. But he's seen the tattoo, that's enough. He's watching me, his face blank, just leaning there.

"Be right back, baby," I say to Paul and walk out. I know Fred's following me, so I just go into his office, trying to figure out how much to tell him.

I sit and stare at the ceiling, waiting for him to say something. And I'm thinking it's really none of his business.

"Both?" he asks, real quiet.

"Yep." I don't look at him, just the ceiling.

"Since when?"

"The beginning."

I can hear his chair creak as he shifts. "Nine months or more. Now you've marked him for you both."

"Yep."

Fred doesn't say anything for a while and then he sighs. "Guess I better get to know the man. Got a feeling a lot of thought went into this."

"Did." I know I'm being an ass to him, and I hate that, but I can't seem to stop. This is fucking scary shit, you know? Almost worse than coming out to my dad.

"Fuck, Gent. Doesn't it get confusing? Loving them

both? Loving twins, for Christ's sake?"

Now I do look at him. "No. They're mine. I'm theirs. All there is to it."

Fred just shakes his head. "You are so gone, man. Gotta hand it to you, you hid it well. Thought Paul was it for you, never thought there would be anyone else in your life. Ever."

"There won't be. We're...three. That's all." I look him in the eye. "Hurts to hide Jamie, though. Can't let anyone know, for obvious reasons. Makes me insane sometimes."

Fred nods. "Yeah, I can imagine. Bet it hurts him too. And you've just committed to a lifetime of that, Gent."

"Committed to more than that."

"Yeah. I know. Now, get out of here and tell your man to keep that tat dry until it's healed over. And Gent?"

"Yeah?"

"Fucking nice job. It's gorgeous."

I grin at him. "Yeah. It's perfect."

And it is.

I wake up when Paul turns around in my arms and leans across me to kiss Jamie. I'm a little smooshed into the mattress, but it's a good feeling, Paul's body on mine, Jamie's pressed into my back. Warm.

I hear them whisper "happy birthday" to each other and then Paul shifts a bit, kisses my jaw until I turn my head enough that he can kiss me. Feather-light kisses across my lips and then Jamie kisses me the same way. "Happy birthday, Gent."

"Happy birthday, baby." I sigh happily and squirm down in the bed, smiling.

"Shit," Jamie groans. Not what I was expecting to

hear.

"What, love?"

"It's late. No time for breakfast, no time for playing, barely enough time to shower." He rolls over and gets out of bed, heading for the bathroom.

I look at the clock. Nine o'clock. Paul's already late, and Jamie's only got half an hour to get to the store. "Damn it."

Paul kisses me again and gets up, grabbing clothes and throwing them on. "I gotta go. Fuck, I'm sorry, Gent. Listen, supper tonight—I'll call you and tell you where we've got reservations, meet us there." He kisses me again and he's gone. I hear him call an "I love you" out and I guess it doesn't matter if it's for Jamie or me. He loves us both.

When Jamie's showered and gone I get up and call the jeweler. Paul's present is ready, so I pick it up on my way to work. Fred tells me Paul called and hands me the address of the restaurant, says it's okay if I take off right after my last scheduled client so I can get there on time. Sort of a birthday present.

As it is I get there after the boys and when I get to the table, they've already started on the bottle of wine. I sit down and we all sort of grin at each other.

We chat for a couple of minutes about our day, and then there's a hand on my leg, moving up to my lap real fast. I look at Paul and wink, then sort of get lost in his eyes. Can hardly see any green at all. God, he's about to go off right here and no one's even doing anything. I raise an eyebrow and slip my hand into his lap under the tablecloth. Not only is he hard, but Jamie's hand is already there, teasing him.

"Let's go," I say. "Order pizza or something."

They don't even say anything, just stand up and head for the door, pulling their coats around them as they go. I apologize to the maitre d' and give him a twenty. When I get outside we all pile into the back seat of a cab and tell the driver to step on it.

Not sure how we make it home fully clothed, but we do. Actually, by the time we get home Paul seems calmer, and we just sort of wander into the living room and take off our jackets and stand there for a minute, looking at each other.

I can't believe how much I love them. They're kind and smart and giving and warm, and I'm stunned by the sheer and utter beauty of them every fucking day. My boys. And one of them even has my name on him.

I'm not sure who moves first. Maybe it's me, maybe it's them together. It doesn't matter. All that matters is that we're together now, arms around each other, three mouths kissing and tasting and giving, low moans and sounds of love in my ears and the flavors of them together on my tongue. Heaven.

We kiss like that until we are breathless and then we just stand there a moment longer, foreheads together.

"Happy birthday," I whisper. They answer me with soft kisses.

Paul finally pulls us all out of it, his eyes glittering. "Presents!"

Jamie looks at me and I nod, go back to get my coat. When I turn around, the slim box in my hand, Jamie looks at Paul and says, "Let's do this in the bedroom. Get naked, lay back and be happy?"

Paul blinks, then he smiles slowly and puts his hand to Jamie's back. "Examine all the presents real close?"

Jamie grins and heads to the bedroom, Paul and me close behind him.

I set the box on the nightstand and watch as Paul unbuttons Jamie's shirt. So pretty together. I remember I need to get the small pliers from the toolbox in the kitchen and head out of the room. They're naked and waiting for me when I get back, standing in front of the full-length mirror.

Jamie is standing behind Paul, arms around his twin's waist, and Paul's leaning back on him. I can see Jamie's tattoo and Paul's piercings. Time to make our claim on Paul. I set the pliers down next to the bed and take off my clothes. By the time I'm done my boys are moving to the bed and we all sort of stretch out, lying on our stomachs. My leg is tangled with Jamie's and I put a hand over his tattoo as I kiss him.

"Ready, pretty?"

"For ages now." I kiss Paul and reach out for the box, set it down in front of him. "Happy birthday, baby."

Paul kisses me and then Jamie. He looks at the box and rips the paper off with eager fingers, but stops before he opens it. I nod at him, and then Jamie nudges him with an elbow. "Come on, baby. Not gonna hurt."

He lifts the lid and I swear he gasps. Jamie just stares. He'd seen the sketches, but not the chain. It's fine gold, thick enough not to snap, big enough to play with, but not heavy enough to bother him. And in the center is an interlocking 'J' and 'G'.

Paul picks it up and fingers it for a second and flips over on his back. "Put it on, now, please!"

I laugh and reach for the pliers and open the rings on the ends of the chain. I lace his nipple rings through them and carefully squeeze them closed, then give the chain a gentle tug, making him gasp again.

He smiles at us, eyes dilating, his cock filling between his legs. "Jamie, get Gent's. Want to play."

Jamie kisses him and reaches for the chain, brushing his fingers over Paul's nipple as his hand moves. "Yeah. Want to play, too."

He gets off the bed and goes to the dresser while I

kiss Paul, reveling in the soft noises he's already making. Jamie comes back and curls up against my side, pushing into our kiss for a moment before placing a box on my chest. I look at it, surprised.

I don't know why, but I never even thought about what they might get me. I guess I was too wrapped up in the tattoo and arranging for the chain. In any case, seeing the tiny box makes my breath come faster, makes my chest ache. I'm almost afraid to open it.

There's a bow on top so I stick it on Paul's head, making him laugh. They both sit up and watch me as I take the paper off, and I glance at them when I see the jeweler's name on the cardboard box. They look back, happy and hopeful, and I smile as I lift the lid. There's another box in the cardboard one, a small leather covered box with a hinged lid that creaks a little when I open it.

They gave me their father's ring. And where there had been a faded ivy leaf, there's now an elegantly carved "G". I'm not sure how long I stare at it before I look up at them, but when I look I think I'm never going to be able to look away. Green eyes meet mine with an intensity I haven't seen before.

"Ours."

"Yours."

Jamie takes the box from me. My hands are shaking as Paul slips the ring on the third finger of my left hand.

Taken.

Paul laces his fingers with mine, and Jamie's twist around our clasped hands. I'm trying to blink away tears when one of them kisses me, and everything dissolves into love and passion and need; everything in the world swept away except them and me.

Forever.

Chapter Sixteen

It's Saturday night and I'm really happy to finally be home. I swear, if I have to ink any more daggers with serpents wrapped around them on any more smelly guys with beer guts I'll puke. But then, at least I'm back to working almost full time at the parlor and off the beer-pulling gig. That was worse. Usually.

It wasn't a good night. Lots of clients, but they were all either half drunk and ugly 'cause we wouldn't do their work, getting crap from the wall done, or trolling. I didn't help myself much either. One guy kicked a fuss 'cause I don't have ink on my arms or anywhere else he could see.

"How come you don't have tattoos? How can you be good at what you do without experiencing it?" he asked.

I skipped the whole bit about how someone can be very good at doing something like this without actually getting it done and just answered the first question. "I do. I've got two, they're just hidden."

"Ugly?"

"Fuck, no. They'd blow your mind, but they aren't

in a spot I show off to just anyone." As soon as I say it I know he's gonna demand to see them. And he does.

"I want to see them."

"No."

"Why not?"

I was ready to just let the guy go. Don't want to work on someone like that, my tats are none of his business, you know? But Fred was in the room and he was kind of laughing. He knows where they are, though he's only seen one of them. Hell, he did that one for me.

I rolled my eyes. "Because I'm not gonna fucking drop my pants for you. Now, you want to do this or not?"

Guy sulked, but he settled back and let me draw the dragon he wanted on his biceps. He didn't say anything until I was done.

"Why the hell would you get a tattoo on your ass?"

Fred laughed. "He didn't."

Guy looked at me and blinked. "Fuck. That had to hurt."

I just nodded and took his money.

So when I get home I'm grumpy and tired and just want to curl up on the couch with my boys and watch TV. Or maybe we can watch TV in bed. I'm easy.

They're in the living room when I get home, and I can tell something's up. Well, two somethings, but I'll skip the details, 'cept to say that they're at least fully clothed, just making out like they're almost ready to move on to the getting naked part.

I stand there and watch for a couple of minutes. My boys are just so amazing together. Paul's on top of Jamie, and that's a treat to watch—Paul's not usually that aggressive with him. I think that in the whole year and a bit we've been together I've only seen Paul do Jamie about a dozen times.

But Paul's wild tonight, kissing Jamie hard before

moving to suck on his neck, hands on Jamie's hips to pull him in hard while he grinds against him. Fucking hot.

Jamie groans and arches his back, stretching out under Paul's weight. His eyes flutter open and he sees me. He gives me a slow grin and moves against Paul, making Paul moan in this needy, breathless way that sends a jolt to my cock. Yeah, I'm hard already, getting off on watching my boys.

"Gent's home, Paul. Time to start the party."

Paul moans into his neck.

"Looks like you've already started," I say with a grin.

Jamie rolls his eyes and tries to get Paul off him. He finally just pushes him onto the floor. "Nah, just getting him warmed up."

I look at Paul, sprawled on the floor. His eyes are dark, his lips red and swollen. His hard-on is easy to see in his tight jeans. "Looks warm," I say, and Jamie snickers as he sits up on the couch.

"Yeah. Boy's on fire tonight. Real hungry."

Paul doesn't say anything, just gets on all fours and crawls over to me, then sits back on his heels and reaches for my fly. I look down at him, get lost in those green eyes and just stand there while he undoes my pants and eases my cock out. His tongue flicks out and licks me, then his hands are on my hips, holding me tight while he sucks me in.

"Christ. Oh baby, that's nice." I watch him for a second and then look at Jamie. He's sitting on the couch, frozen, watching. I can see the muscles on his shoulders twitch. "What got into him? Not that I'm complaining." I moan softly and look back down at Paul as I feel his teeth scrape lightly on the up stroke.

I can hear Jamie's zipper. "He got a promotion. Wants to celebrate."

Paul moves a hand to my balls and I thrust into his

mouth a little. He starts to suck hard, and I can feel his fingers teasing me, his tongue driving me fucking crazy.

"We can... oh God... we can do that."

Then I can't say anything as Paul takes me in all the way. When the hell did he learn to do that? Doesn't matter, all that matters is the wet heat of his mouth and the gentle fingers on my balls and the way he's swallowing around the head of my cock.

"Shit, baby... gonna come soon."

He groans and I can feel it in my spine, and something important explodes at the back of my skull. I thrust hard, can't help it, and then I'm coming down his throat.

"Fuck, yes. Oh God. Paul. Oh God."

He swallows it all and then he lets me go, lets me fall back onto the chair. I almost make it too, but land mostly on the floor when my legs give out. My eyes aren't real focused but I see him spin, still on his knees and he's got his mouth on Jamie now, sucking him off fast and hard, like he hadn't already done me.

Jamie's head falls back and he just jerks his hips, shoves his cock deep into Paul's mouth. They've been hungry for a while I guess, and it only takes about two minutes for Jamie to call out his bother's name and start to come. When he's done Paul licks him clean and then falls back on the floor.

I'm still feeling pretty boneless, but the man just did a fucking fabulous job and deserves a reward, right? So I lie down next to him and kiss him deep, taste Jamie and me and fuck if that doesn't make my dick twitch.

"Fuck, baby. You're on tonight. What do you want? Want to fuck? Get fucked? Anything you want, love."

Jamie chuckles from the couch and rolls off to join us on the floor, his hand going to stroke Paul through his jeans. "He knows what he wants. Already said I'd do it, but he wanted you to watch."

I raise a brow. My baby is a kinky man. Lord knows what he wants this time. I kiss Paul again and lean up to kiss Jamie. Paul's moaning and thrusting his cock into Jamie's hand.

"So what does our boy need tonight?" I ask Jamie.

I'm undoing Paul's jeans and Jamie's working at the buttons on his shirt. "He wants a good hard spanking."

I blink. We've done that before. Granted not in a few months, but it's not a new kink. I'm kind of getting used to Paul springing new kinks on us. Well, nothing wrong with the tried and true, I suppose. It certainly gets him off.

I nod and kiss Paul again, just brush my lips across his. "Whatever you want."

Paul moans. "Want it, Gent. Need it. Need you to see."

I smile at him and then Jamie and I strip off his clothes. He's so fucking hot. Beautiful body, lying on the floor. Looks like some art shot. Light hair, green eyes, and that amazing cock hard and curved up to his stomach. I lean down and lick at his balls, make him twitch and shudder.

"Suck him after, pretty." I look up and see Jamie watching, his eyes as dark as his twins.

Paul springs to life, so to speak, and hauls us off to the bedroom. I'm holding his hand sort of laughing at him and Jamie's got this wide, shit-eating grin on his face.

We get into the bedroom and Paul throws himself across the bed, then just as fast rolls over and looks at us.

"Brush, Jamie? Hand? What do you want?" He looks like a little kid who's just been promised a pony ride at his birthday party. Except for the hard-on. That's nothing a little kid could sport.

Jamie shakes his head and leans down over Paul.

"Calm down, love. It's up to you. What do you want?"

Paul actually looks like he's thinking about it, even though his hand has strayed to his cock. He's stroking himself lightly, his eyes far away, then he shudders softly and looks into Jamie's eyes.

"Want your hand, Jamie. Please?"

Jamie kisses him, soft and slow. There is nothing on this planet prettier than my boys together. I sit on the bed, up by the headboard. I'm just watching this time and suddenly I realize that this *is* a new kink. Not for Paul, but for me. I get off on my twins, always have. Like to watch them kiss, like to watch them love each other. Get off on them separately and together. But when we've done this before, it's just been me and my baby; Jamie wasn't even home the first time.

I really want to watch this.

Jamie pulls away from Paul and gets him settled on the bed, but Paul moves back, draping his body like he did when I spanked him with the brush—ass over the end of the bed, cock just barely able to touch the edge of the bed. Jamie just shrugs and kisses his shoulder then moves over to kiss me hard, his hand going to my half hard cock. "Save that. Want it."

I try to laugh, but I think I moan instead.

Jamie smiles and goes to stand behind Paul. I have no idea how Paul can stand this part, the waiting. I'm sitting all comfy on my ass, he's about to get his beaten, and I'm tense and half wild waiting for Jamie's hand to fall. Paul's looking at me, calm for the first time since I got home. His eyes are clear and he's got this slightly shy smile on, sort of "Oops, you caught me. Sorry to trouble you." He fucking blows me a kiss.

Jamie's hand comes down fast and hard and I jump. Paul's eyes get dark, but he's still watching me, though the smile has faded a bit. When Jamie hits him again the smile vanishes and Paul blinks.

Jamie rains blows down and I start to squirm. He's hitting hard, hard as I did at least. I can't see Paul's ass, but as it goes on I can picture it getting red. Jamie's eyes are sort of glazed, like he's in a trance. Each blow is the same, the same timing, the same force, the same spot.

Paul's eyes lose focus and finally drift shut, his face slack. He's gone. I can see him breathing, deep and steady, see him arch his back for every stroke. He's completely lost in it, and his face looks completely peaceful.

Jamie's on the other hand is starting to look a little fevered. His cock is hard, standing out from his body and his arm is still swinging. His rhythm is amazing, each time he hits Paul it's like a dance, or a complicated play made to look easy. His eyes are huge, and I see so many differences in my boys.

Paul starts to moan and I watch him carefully. His eyes are squeezed shut now, and he's worrying his lower lip with his teeth. He grunts as Jamie connects and I see him try to talk. After a few tries he finally whispers, "More."

My cock fucking leaps and I wrap my hand around the base hard to stop from coming. Jamie hits him harder and faster and my hips are pumping, keeping in time with them. Paul looks blissed out and I can see him getting close. I glance up at Jamie, catch his eye and nod.

Jamie hits him again, lower.

"Yes!"

Jamie does it again, and keeps doing it. Paul's not moving anymore, just taking it, and I can see blood on his lips. His eyes snap open and he stares at me. I think he's here now, back with us.

"Now," he says in a normal tone of voice, and then he's shooting hard, streams of come soaking the sheets in front of him. His eyes roll back in his head and he starts to cry.

Jamie kneels down behind him, holds on. He looks at me, his eyes wide and needy. "Gent." His voice is harsh, raw.

I move around the bed to them and kiss Paul gently. Jamie waits his turn, pushes his tongue down my throat and fucks my mouth with it. "Need you. Now, please, God please, pretty."

I don't waste a lot of time while I find a rubber. I get behind him and bite his shoulder as he spreads his legs for me. It isn't until I touch his cock that I realize he's already come, spent himself spanking Paul or watching him shoot. I slick my hand with the come on his legs and open him with two fingers, then push my cock in, deep and hard.

He screams, head back on my shoulder. "Fuck yeah. Do it. Christ, so good."

I take him for his word and thrust into him again and again, just trying to get off, need to be with him like this, intense and hungry and needy and now.

I've been wired for ages, since before he started spanking Paul, and I can't last long. Don't need to. I'm pushing him forward with every thrust, and he's got his arms braced on either side of Paul, trying not to crush Paul's ass with his body.

I pound into his ass and feel him clench around me.

"Shit! Gonna shoot, love." Then I'm coming, cock pulsing in him and he groans, this harsh, deep sound that turns into a sigh.

I ease out of him and lie on the floor, wait until I can breathe again before crawling up to kiss them. Paul's eyes are starting to clear and Jamie's trying to get him to get on the bed. We all manage to get there and wrap around each other, exchanging intense deep kisses that say more than we ever can with words.

"I love you, Gent."

Maybe it can be said after all.
"I love you, too."

Chapter Seventeen

It's a pretty calm night at home, except I can't seem to stop moving. Which is causing some trouble, seeing as how I'm laying half on Paul and Jamie's laying on me. It's a good thing our couch is nice and big.

"Gent, cut it out," Paul says. "You move, I move. And it hurts."

I sort of blink up at him. Hurts? Jamie laughs and shifts on top of me, which means that I press into Paul and he winces.

"The day after the spanking is almost as much fun as the spanking," Jamie says as he leers at Paul.

I look at Paul, and he blushes. He's so damn adorable when he blushes. He's wearing the softest pair of sweatpants he has and he's wiggling now, sort of smiling a little.

I grin at him. "Good pain or bad?"

Jamie snorts. "Check it out for yourself, pretty." He takes my hand and puts it in Paul's lap. Apparently it's good pain. I rub at Paul through his pants, making him moan; I can feel him get harder.

Jamie's watching me stroke Paul and he's got this look in his eye that goes right to my cock even faster than feeling Paul hard and hot under my hand. "You're restless tonight. Wanna play?"

"Always," I say. 'Cause it's true. And it keeps me from asking what I want to ask. Not sure it's really what I want.

"What's the game?" Jamie's getting off me now and tugging at my jeans. He gets them open and I lift my hips so he can pull them off.

"Want to watch you and Paul."

I sit up and pull off my shirt, watch Jamie strip down too. He gets Paul to stand up by the easiest way possible—just hauls him to his feet. He pulls off Paul's shirt and plays with his chain while I ease his pants down over his tender ass, pausing to lick it once or twice. Paul shivers and then moans as Jamie slides down his body and licks at his cock.

Paul's back arches a little and I put my hands on his hips, keeping him steady. Jamie just keeps licking his cock like it's ice cream and then Paul drops a hand to his twin's head and fists his hair. I think it's some sort of signal to Jamie, sort of a "fuck, do it now or I'm going to go mad" thing, 'cause Jamie just takes him and sets to work.

I know what Paul's feeling, I get treated to that mouth pretty often and every single fucking time it drives me out of my head. He's something else. He can suck you so hard you think your eyes are going to pop out and it never feels like too much. And he can be so gentle that the teasing alone can make you come, no sucking needed.

"God, yes. Feels so fucking good," Paul moans. My fingers dig into his hips and he surges forward into Jamie's mouth. Jamie groans around his cock and I can feel my hard-on twitch in response.

Paul's ass is still kinda pink looking, which surprises

me. Actually, I'm surprised he doesn't have bruises. I let go of his hip with one hand and stroke his ass gently, feel him quiver at my touch.

I touch him again, gently. Every time I brush my fingers over him he shakes and moans, and I'm just so fucking hard. I want to know.

I look at Jamie, his mouth around Paul's cock, taking him in deep. He's jerking off now, and I can't wait until they're done. I just...can't.

"Jamie, I want you to spank me."

"Fuck! Jamie!" Paul screams out and then he thrusts deep and they're both coming, Paul shooting into Jamie's mouth and Jamie coming all over the floor.

"Jesus, Gent," is the first thing Paul can say. "Warn me next time. I just about fell over."

Jamie's sprawled out on the floor, staring at me. "You sure?"

I just nod.

"Where?"

I look around the living room. "Here's good." I kiss Paul and then I stand up, wait for Jamie to get up. He kisses me hard, one hand on my cock, stroking me lightly.

I move away from him, brace myself on the arm of the couch and wait. Paul's wide-eyed again. He moves to sit on the floor by the chair, already working his erection back to life.

Jamie stands behind me and leans over, kisses a path down my back. Then he goes back up and moves my hair, licks my tattoo. One warm hand is stroking my ass gently, like he's getting to know it all over again. A finger moves between my legs and traces the pattern there.

Then he's gone, and I miss his heat.

I feel it before I hear it. A sharp sting that makes me jump a little. And then the next. I don't jump, but I dig my fingers into the couch. The third is sharp and fast. The fourth hurts. The fifth makes my skin burn, the tingles all melding together. I close my eyes.

It goes on. I know when it's coming and I want the pain to end, but I want the shock of each slap. My cock is aching and my balls are starting to throb with my heartbeat. I think I'm moaning.

Then the pain slides back. It's still there, but it's a snap and then it's heat and then it's bliss. I can feel his hand, feel each finger as it lands. I arch my back, up then down, trying to find the place which feels best, and never quite get there.

The rhythm is hypnotic. The heat is astounding. Jamie is so fucking good at this, I want it to go on and on, but I can feel things speeding up, can feel my heart beating faster, can feel each blow before it lands and I just need something, any little thing to send me over but I don't know what it is.

"More," I hear myself whisper. I vaguely remember Paul asking for more and through the haze I wonder if I'm in the place he goes.

Jamie gives me more. Harder, lower, faster, and I'm chasing it, reaching and reaching, and I think I'm moaning nonsense now, but fuck it feel like I'm going to come apart at the seams and then Paul is there. Under me. I just barely register his presence and then there is white-hot heat and suction around my cock and I come so fucking hard, shoot forever into my boy's throat, hips snapping back and forth 'cause I just can't stop.

I fuck Paul's mouth until I'm spent and then a cool slick finger is in my ass and I know what I need now. What we need.

"Please, Jamie. Fuck me."

Jamie presses into me and it's perfect. One slow stroke that takes him deep and over my prostate and Paul's mouth is still on me, keeping me hard. Jamie fucks me real slow, sliding in and out and brushing his hands over my ass. I can feel the sparks go from my skin to my brain.

We're like that for ages, the three of us moving slowly, coming down as much as building up, and then Paul moans around me and I open my eyes. He's got his hand on his cock and he's moving faster. He comes as I watch, and it sends me over again, without warning. Jamie stills in my ass as I shudder, then he moves, fast and hard, coming for me.

Paul licks me clean and Jamie eases out. I'm shaking, I don't think I can stand. Jamie picks me up and carries me to bed. They clean me up and hold me, tell me they love me, over and over.

"I love you, too. Thank you."

I fall asleep wrapped in my boys, smiling.

Okay, so maybe it's a bit of an obsession, the way I've been thinking about this whole spanking thing. First time I did it to Paul I just let it slide, but after the next time, when Jamie spanked him and I watched, and then when I finally got brave enough to ask Jamie to do it to me...I don't know. I think about it a lot now.

We're all at home, all in bed and almost asleep. Good night kisses have been done and we're all wrapped in each other, Paul nested in my arms and Jamie wrapped around me. We're not asleep, maybe not even near it, and I gotta ask him.

"Jamie?"

"Yeah, pretty?" He sounds wide awake, so I think maybe we can talk about it without anyone getting to thinking and not being able to get back to that happy almost asleep place.

"You ever wanted to get spanked? I mean, I know you get off on the doing, just wondered if you would ever get into the receiving."

Right away I know it was the wrong thing to say. He doesn't pull away or anything, but Paul gets stiff in my arms, and not in the good way. I feel Jamie shake his head behind me.

"Not any more, pretty. Don't bottom well, if you hadn't noticed."

And yeah, I noticed. He gets off on being fucked, sucks like a demon, but it's not the same. When he's on his knees he's still in charge, when I'm in him I'm not topping him, I'm just with him. He's not in charge, exactly, he just isn't...under anyone's control. Ever.

I nod my head and let it go, ready to let it drop, for Paul's sake, if nothing else. My boy is still tense, and I give him a squeeze, let him know I'm not going to push it, not going to do anything to make anyone hurt over this. He relaxes a bit and I kiss his shoulder, then turn my head to kiss Jamie.

His kiss is quick and light, sort of distracted. He's looking at the ceiling. "Asked for it once or twice," he says in a low voice.

Paul shifts in my arms. "Jamie, don't."

"Shh. 'S okay, Paul. I'm not gonna go there. Relax."

I get Paul to lean into me again, figure that it's over and whatever happened before me is done and gone and doesn't have a place in our bed.

Jamie nestles into me again and I can feel his arm wrap all the way over me to rest on Paul's hip. No one says anything for a long while, and I think Paul's even fallen asleep.

"Gent?"

"Yeah, love?"

"You can know if you want. I'll tell you."

"I know you would, Jamie. But I don't need to. Know it's not your thing, know that something hurt you. Not gonna take you back to that."

Paul sighs and rolls over, pressed into me, a hand reaching to stroke Jamie's face. "I'm still sorry."

"Wasn't you, love. You know that."

"My fault, though."

Jamie shakes his head. "Not. Wasn't then, isn't now. asn't even his fault, and Christ knows he's sorry too." He kisses the palm of Paul's hand and says, "All done and over, baby. And now we're in that good place again, everyone gets what they need. Right?"

Paul nods and kisses him, then kisses me. Jamie pushes in and we're all together; they make sure I'm a part of the resolution. Which is damn kind of them, seeing as how I brought it up.

Paul rolls back to rest his back to my chest and we settle back the way we were. The way we sleep best.

Jamie lifts his hand and brushes my hair out of the way. When he's got the back of my neck bared to him he licks me and starts to suck on my tattoo there, right under my hairline at the top of my spine.

"Why?" he asks, and I haven't got a clue what he means, so I don't answer.

"Why here, why your neck. Why is it hidden?"

"Because it's a part of me that I don't want to share with the world. A part that I needed to reinforce for myself, but not so every jerkoff could see it. It's…it's like I needed to manifest that part of myself, make it outer, but keep it personal."

He nods against my skin, and I think he gets it. He's still sucking on it, I can feel his teeth scrape the skin. I know he's raising a mak, obliterating the tattoo. But it's going to be there when the bruise heals. He knows that, too.

Chapter Eighteen

I walk in the door to our place and stop dead. One of my boys—and yeah, I know which one—has gone a little nuts with the fake spider webs and other Halloween shit.

"Paul?" I call out, making my way down the hall, pushing the silly stuff out of my way with just about every step. "You better be done, baby, 'cause this is getting out of hand."

"So take me in hand," he says, his voice coming from the bedroom.

I laugh. Always eager, my boy.

I walk into the bedroom, see Paul lying on his stomach watching TV. "Where's Jamie?"I slide a hand over his back and kiss his warm mouth, happy to be home.

"Mmm. He's getting something for you, be back in a minute." He pushes up into my hand, his own fingers going to my hair as he kisses me again. He's hungry, his tongue is impatient as it slides on mine.

"For me? Why?"

Paul's eyes are glittering. "Halloween. Needed

something for the costumes."

I step back and look at him. He's practically writhing on the bed, twisting and turning and pretty much on his way to rubbing off. Whatever my boys have planned has Paul wound up so tight he's about to blow just thinking about it.

"Baby? Are we going out or staying in?" I'm open to both, but by the way Paul's humping the bed, starting to make helpless "need to come now" noises and everything,I'm leaning toward just staying home and fucking him senseless. After I watch him for a bit.

An arm slinks around my waist and Jamie's there, his tongue in my ear. "Out, pretty. You're taking us out." Then his other arm comes over my shoulder and he shows off what he's got for me.

Leashes.

"Fuck, yes!" Paul fucking bucks on the bed and comes in his jeans, eyes wide.

"Oh, *very* nice, baby," Jamie purrs. He goes over to Paul and kisses him hard, fucking his mouth with his tongue.

I'm just standing there, sort of lost. Really turned on, but wondering where the hell I'm supposed to take horny identical twins on leashes. The mental image doesn't even get fully formed before I'm stripping off my pants and landing on the bed. I mean, *fuck*.

Jamie's mouth is on my cock, wet and hot and so fucking good; Paul's kissing me, his tongue sliding over my teeth and he's sucking on my lower lip. I thrust my hips a couple of times and Jamie sucks me hard, his fingers holding my hips and digging into my ass as I shoot into his throat.

"Holy shit," I gasp when Paul lets my mouth go.

"Yeah, pretty." Jamie's breathless, his pants open and riding down as Paul works his cock with his hand. Jamie arches, spraying his own shirt with come and we all sort of collapse on the bed, panting.

"Jesus. We may not live to actually go anywhere," I say, only half kidding. "Where the fuck am I supposed to take you?"

Turns out Paul—of course—knows a place. It's a club, supposed to be pretty swank, and they tend to let just about anything go. Twins on leashes will get looks, but no one's gonna freak. Especially 'cause it's Halloween.

Can get away with just about anything on Halloween.

We all climb into the shower and I set to finding out more about what they have planned.

"Leashes? What am I supposed to clip 'em to?"

Jamie grins at me over Paul's shoulder as they rub up against each other, water and soap making them slide together real easy. "Collars."

My mind blanks for a second and I start stroking my cock, not even really realizing it. "Yeah?"

"Yeah," Paul sighs, moving faster against Jamie. "And we got you stuff to wear, too."

I blink and lean back against the wall, watching them. Jamie hooks one of Paul's legs over his hip and eases him back so he's leaning on the other wall. I speed up my hand and watch Jamie guide his cock along Paul's ass.

"Oh God, yes, Jamie. Love me." Paul's head falls back and Jamie pushes into him.

"Fuck, so tight, baby. Ride me."

I stand there in the steam, fucking my hand as I watch my beautiful boys love each other, Jamie's hips moving fast and hard. "Christ, you two are hot," I groan, watching Paul's eyes roll up in his head as Jamie fucks him. Paul's braced on the wall as Jamie moves in him, one hand stroking his own cock. He's whimpering and groaning and Jamie's panting, and I feel myself getting close. Paul opens his eyes wide and Jamie whispers, "Come for me, baby boy." Paul cries out.

I smell Paul's come, see him shoot. Jamie freezes and then grunts, pushing in hard and then he's coming too, and it's just too much. I shudder, my back arching as I thrust into my hand, cock fucking throbbing as I shoot my load.

We manage to find one another, share wet sloppy kisses, all tongue and no coordination. When we catch our breath and finish in the shower the boys tell me to go to the bedroom and get dressed, to meet them out front. They don't want me to see the full effect of their costumes until we get to the club.

I shake my head, but do as I'm told. Paul's got a box of stuff ready for me, so I dry my hair, slicking it back tight, and get dressed. Tight leather pants that I haven't worn in a year, 'cause they're *too* tight. Biker boots. A black T-shirt that's new but about two sizes too small. Can see my nipple rings and my chain through it. Black leather jacket that I usually wear when we go to the Edge. I stuff the leashes in my pocket with a shudder of anticipation and head out.

I stop at the bathroom door and bang on it. "You two almost ready?"

Jamie calls out that they need about two more minutes, get a cab to wait, so I just head down and flag one. They come out just a minute later, so they couldn't have had much to do.

They're wearing their usual jackets and black fucking tight shiny pants with combat boots, and their eyes are rimmed with black kohl. Hurt me.

Paul gives the cabby the address and we all ignore each other on the way there. I'm so fucking hard already, and we've already come twice tonight. We get to play again and I swear it'll last all night.

We get to the club and I pay the driver, wait for my boys on the curb. I lead the way in, and Paul's right, it's a really nice place. The music is loud without being earsplitting, and it's pretty well lit, though there looks to be dark corners, which I'm thinking is going to come in real handy. There's an honest to God coat check room so we stop and hand 'em over.

I peel off my leather and take the leashes out, standing back to see my boys. They look at me, two sets of black-lined green eyes, hot and horny and waiting to see what I do. They move together, unzipping their jackets.

I think I forget to breathe for a few seconds, and I know my jaw drops open.

Neither one of them has a shirt on. Tight, black PVC pants, low on their hips. Paul with his nipple rings and chain, Jamie's tattoo fucking glowing on his back. They're *shiny*, gleaming with oil, every cut muscle standing out, nipples dark and hard, matching their clear as shit hard-ons. Around their necks they have wide black leather collars on with D rings at the front.

When I remember to breathe I clip the leashes on them and feel them shudder. The guy who took the coats is staring. I just grin at him and lead my boys into the club.

There's a lot of people there, mostly on the wooden dance floor. The rest of the flooring is this deep red plush carpeting, and there're all these tables everywhere, and a few booths. Everyone is in some sort of costume, ranging from the typical superhero/knight/Zorro shit to people in leather and lace. There're a couple of girls dressed as angels, with big white feathery wings and gold haloes, and another group of about five people dressed as a bunch of grapes. Pretty funny.

I walk along the edge of the dance floor, leading my twins on their leashes. People stop dancing and stare. I glance back and have to grin; Paul and Jamie are holding hands. They look unbelievable, shiny and hard and so fucking sexy. I decide we better dance, 'cause if I get them into a booth I'm not letting them out.

I walk to the center of the floor and people move out of the way. I hear someone ask Jamie a question and Jamie just shakes his head. "I'm his," he says, and points to me. My cock throbs.

I turn and face them, still holding the leashes in my hand. I wind the extra length around my wrist, bringing them closer to me, my hips catching the beat of the music, tuning out everything but my boys and the need to move with them. When they get close enough I kiss Paul, hold his head by the back of the neck and just thrust my tongue down his throat. When I let him go I look at Jamie and realize, all of a sudden, that I've never kissed him in public. Ever. And definitely not when everyone would see that we're all together.

I pull Jamie in tight, letting the leashes loosen so Paul can move away, let him slide behind Jamie. I hold onto Jamie's hips and grind into him, feel his cock pushing against mine and then I attack his mouth, claim him right there on the dance floor, in front of about two hundred people.

His arms wrap around me and he kisses back; I can hear him sob into my mouth. Our hips are moving with the music, we're dancing and fucking and loving, and Paul's hands are sliding over my back, wrapping around from behind Jamie, trapping Jamie between us.

I break away from Jamie's mouth and kiss Paul, leaning around Jamie, pulling him tighter to me. Paul's slinking up and down Jamie's back, I can tell he's rubbing off on Jamie's ass and everyone else can too. I can hear someone moan and it takes me a minute to realize that it isn't one of us, it's the guy beside us.

I look over and he's leaning on his boyfriend, back to

chest. They both have a hand down the front guy's pants, jerking him off while they watch us. I blink and then turn back to my boys, kiss Jamie again and whisper "Love you" against his mouth.

He moves against me again and I step to the side, pull on the leases until I can turn Jamie around so they're facing each other, and I'm against Jamie's back. God, they are so sleek, the oil in their skin making them smooth and hot and slippery. I put my arms around Jamie, pull Paul in by his hips. When they touch they both hiss, and Paul's eyes are fucking wild, glazing over with need. They press tight together and Jamie's got his hands on Paul's ass and we're all humping on the dance floor, only our pants keeping us from actually fucking right there.

"Kiss him," I order, and it doesn't matter who I'm telling. I have my boys out for the night and I'm fucking showing them off.

Paul and Jamie start to kiss and grind and the guy beside us comes in his pants with a near scream, and then his partner hauls him away. Guess he's about to take it up the ass in one of those dark corners.

Other people are watching too, and there's a lot of groping going on. My boys are bringing the place to its knees; literally. From where I am I can see at least three blowjobs, either in progress against the wall or about to happen in one of the booths.

"Fuck, we gotta go somewhere." It's Jamie, and I'll admit I thought it would be Paul needing it. But then, Paul's nodding his head, his hips moving rhythmically against Jamie.

"Gent, please. Gonna fucking come right here, I swear."

I slide a hand down in between them and just about come myself. I can feel the silky smooth skin of Jamie's cock; he's so hard he's actually pushing out of his pants, and I can feel the pre-come gathering at the tip.

"Oh fuck, pretty, please," he whimpers.

"Oh, love," I breathe. "Want you." I let the leashes off my wrist and turn, walking away, leading my boys off the floor. I hear another groan, but don't stop to see who it is. Enough of a show for one night, it's time to make my boys all mine again.

We head to the back of the club and suddenly the booths and tables give way and it's dark, the light dimmed to that equivalent to a night light. There's hanging curtains against the wall and I pull one back, hoping there's a back hall or something so I don't have to take my boys into the john to get off. It's just a small alcove, no furniture or anything, only about two feet deep. Jamie pushes me in and has my pants unzipped before I can even think of moving on.

He's on his knees in front of me, and Paul's beside me, both of them with their hands everywhere. I turn my head and kiss Paul, get his cock free of his pants and start stroking him off with quick strokes, just about coming on the spot when Jamie finally takes me in his mouth.

"Oh shit. Go easy, love, don't want to blow too soon," I manage.

He hums something agreeable and backs off a bit, his hand going to his own zipper.

"Show me, Jamie. Show me your cock," Paul says, his voice tight. I groan and Jamie pulls out his prick, starts stroking off in the dim light.

I can't take much more. It's like one long tease, and I finally snap. I reach down and haul him up, spin him into the wall. "Jamie?"

"Yeah, pretty. Don't ask, just do it."

I hold onto his hips hard and pray that I'm slick enough from his spit that I won't hurt him and push into his ass, as slow as I can. But, fuck, he's so tight and hot and I want him so bad, want to just plough into his ass and make him scream.

Paul's hands are tugging at my nipple rings and he's whispering filthy shit in my ear about how we look, about how he was leaking so much on the dance floor that the inside of his pants are slick, about how hard it made him to kiss Jamie in front of all those people and I just fucking thrust into Jamie, push myself in until my balls slap up against his ass.

"Oh God, yes," Jamie moans, and Paul's got one hand on Jamie's cock and one on his own and he's pulling them off, so sweet and hard.

I hold onto Jamie's hips and guide him back, find a rhythm in the music and just get lost in the heat and the slide and the steady pressure of it all. He's so tight around me, so hot and perfect and I fuck him hard, feel every groan and sigh and hear every word of love and lust and need.

Paul comes first and I can feel his spunk splash over my hands, over Jamie's hips and then Paul drops to his knees, still shuddering and fucking sucks Jamie in. Jamie makes a long choking sound and his ass clamps around me hard, then he starts to buck, fucking Paul's mouth, riding my cock until he comes, pulling me with him. I come for ages, every twitch of Jamie's making my orgasm last longer and longer, I just shoot over and over until the world goes grey at the edges.

We all sort of tumble to the floor and lay there panting for a long time before we even move enough to kiss each other, let alone put ourselves away. Paul sighs into my ear and licks at my neck and Jamie's curled around me.

"Pretty?" Jamie says, his hand curling around my hip.

"Yeah, love?" I say, but it turns into a squeak when he cups my balls and squeezes gently. Fuck, there is no way any of us is getting it up again, not unless we nap first and oh holy hell, Jamie starts whispering about the people around us and how anyone could literally trip on us and how he wants to fuck where anyone can see and Paul's moaning and pushing into us and trying to kiss Jamie at the same time.

Paul shifts down and starts licking at Jamie's prick and I'm getting hard again watching him tease the head with the tip of his tongue, fucking the slit and then licking all over. My legs fall open and Jamie's fingers play over my balls and tease at my hole, and Paul's sucking him off so prettily…

I groan and let my head fall back, just feel them move over me and listen to the people all around us, and feel the music throbbing, or is that my cock? And shit I just *need* so much. Paul's off Jamie then and kissing my mouth, and I can taste them both, Jamie light and hidden in Paul's mouth, behind the tongue sliding over mine.

"Wanna fuck you, Gent," my baby says in my ear, and I don't even answer, just roll over onto all fours and offer my ass to him, waiting for Jamie to move around so I can suck his dick. Perfect.

My boys in me. Jamie hard and silky in my mouth. Paul -- oh God yes, so goddamn hard oh it hurts with no lube, but it's better and good now and he's going easy and there's fucking spots in front of my eyes and nothing matters but the feel of the slide and press, and oh so full of them, my lovers, my heart and soul, my completion and if he just gets to that one spot one more time I'm going to fucking go off and oh fuck Jamie, yes come for me love, fill me you taste so good, and Paul there there there there oh fuck yes coming coming, oh God yes!

Then there is nothing but space and time and light, and…light? Oh. Audience. The guy just blinks and lets the curtain fall and we all sort of laugh and collapse again. I don't think I'm going to move for the rest of the night, but we gotta. Can't sit here all naked and sticky on the floor of some club I can't even remember the name of.

Eventually we decide it's time to get something to drink, and hell, the night is still young. We can dance again, and maybe see what else happens. Personally, I'm thinking home, bed, sleep.

I'm leading them back to an empty booth when a hand comes down on my arm. It's a big guy with dark hair and fire in his eyes, dressed like Robin Hood.

"Yeah?"

He looks at the twins and sticks his jaw out at them. "They real?"

I look him in the eye. "Real? They're human. They're twins. What else you want to know?"

He looks at me a bit more carefully. "They together?"

Now, that's touchy, but considering the display we made on the dance floor, and just now for anyone how wanted to look, I think I'm going with the truth. "Not just a show."

He nods. "Five hundred."

"Fuck off." Yeah, right. I start to move away but his hand comes back.

"Seven. One hour. No one gets hurt."

I stop, Jamie and Paul on either side of me, for once keeping their mouths shut. "No. They aren't for rent." My voice is hard as steel. Not a fucking chance does anyone get near my boys.

He looks at them again, and his eyes are getting a little desperate. He licks his lips. "Thousand dollars, all night though."

I hit him. Hard right to his jaw, don't even let go of the leashes.

His head snaps back and he stumbles, hits the floor

hard. I stand over him. My voice is harsh and raspy, and I'm breathing hard, starting to shake. "They're mine. No one touches them."

I ditch the leashes and grab their hands, dragging them through the club to the door before a brawl can start. Guy doesn't follow.

We get our coats and fucking run out, and I'm still shaking. Jamie grabs me and pushes me into outside wall of the club. "Pretty. Stop, just calm down."

I look at him. I'm mad and I'm scared and I can't believe that just happened. I grab him by the neck and kiss him hard. He moans into my mouth and then Paul's pulling at us, dragging us down the street. He's hailing a cab.

We pile in and I wrap myself around Jamie. "Sorry. I didn't think, I didn't mean to make it like that. Didn't want people to see you as a freak, just wanted to be open for once, I'm so sorry—"

Jamie kisses me to shut me up and then he turns my head so he can whisper in my ear.

"Pretty, no matter where we go, people are going to want twins. But you made it all right. You made it all right for me to kiss our baby, you made it all right to be together, even it it's just once like that, where people could see. And you made it clear who we all belong to." He pulls away and looks at me steadily.

"Love you, Gent. More than ever."

And it's not okay, but it's better and he's mine and I'm his and it doesn't matter if there are collars or leashes or any other crap tying us all together. 'Cause we're bound by something real.

Chris Owen

Gemini

Printed in the United States
211251BV00009BA/2/P

9 781603 706032